HEIR OF THE FAE

LINSEY HALL

For my mother and all my aunts. I want to make it clear to everyone that my mom and aunts are amazing and nothing like the ones in this book. Honestly it was a little weird to write their scenes. Mom and aunts, this is not about you guys. You are the best. I love you!

1

THE COOL NIGHT AIR BLEW MY HAIR BACK FROM MY FACE AS I crouched in the alley, waiting for my prey. The Council of Demon Slayers had sent me after an Exurbia demon, and it was the perfect night for hunting.

If I ignored the puddle of vomit to my left.

And the spoiled Thai takeout to my right.

It all reeked, making my stomach turn.

I had a strong stomach. After all, I cut into my veins daily as part of my Blood Sorcery.

But vomit was where I drew the line.

I also drew the line at demons who screwed with my city. Which left me in this unfortunate predicament. This demon was coming to steal the magic from unwitting citizens. By doing so, he'd pretty much be stealing their souls.

Not on my watch.

Which meant I was crouched here in the third level of

hell, hoping the demon hurried up so I could kill him and get on with my night.

Movement on a rooftop to my left caught my eye.

What the hell?

It was after three in the morning on the quieter side of town. No one should be out at this hour.

But there was definitely a man up there—tall, broad-shouldered, and with a silhouette that made him look like a god. The moon shone from behind, casting him in shadow, but I couldn't help but think of Tarron.

Tarron, the powerful and devastatingly handsome Fae king who believed I was his fated mate.

Tarron, the same Fae king who'd just learned that I was Unseelie to his Seelie. In Fae terms, I was evil to his good. Dark to his light.

It wasn't a problem for me. I'd been a Dragon Blood all my life, possessing such powerful magic that I could turn to the dark side any time I wanted, becoming obsessed with power.

I never had though.

So learning that I was half Unseelie Fae wasn't that big a deal. To me, at least.

I knew I wouldn't turn evil.

Tarron didn't. And the Unseelie had basically killed his brother. Worse, even.

When he'd found out what I was last week, the disgust on his face had made me run. We'd had something between us—something new but real—and his sudden change of heart...

Yeah, no. Not for me.

I wasn't going to stick around with a guy who thought my origin was disgusting. True, I had no control over my new wings or whatever Unseelie magic existed within me. I hadn't been able to make the wings appear again after they'd shown up the first time, and that was terrifying. But that didn't make me evil.

The figure on the roof didn't move.

Was it really him?

There was no way he'd be spying on me. Not a king, come to the real world of Magic's Bend to watch a peon like myself.

He disappeared, but the tension didn't fade from my shoulders. Just the idea that it might have been him tied me up in knots.

I turned my attention back to the street, just in time to see the demon. He was slinking out of the alley across the street, his form tall and wiry. His skin was a pale, ashy blue and his eyes a brilliant red. Long horns protruded from his head, and his magic reeked of a skunk who'd gone to town in a dumpster.

I grimaced, then frowned.

He didn't look like an Exurbia demon. Maybe he just looked funny? Anyway, he was a demon in the right place at the right time.

Good enough for me.

I called upon my bow and arrow, drawing them from the ether.

The demon was quick, moving toward the open

window of a first-floor apartment. The person who lived there had clearly been trying to catch a bit of breeze.

Instead, they'd catch a demon.

Not tonight.

I rose silently, sighting my arrow and releasing it toward the demon. It flew through the air, swiftly and silently.

A satisfied grin spread across my face.

It'd be a direct hit.

At the last moment, the demon turned and smacked the arrow out of the way. He moved as a blur.

The bastard.

Exurbia demons shouldn't be that fast.

Yeah, he *definitely* wasn't an Exurbia demon.

I raised my bow and arrow again, but his flame red eyes met mine. He grinned, his fangs glinting in the light, then shot a blast of electric blue energy at me. It sparkled with green lights. I'd never seen anything like it.

I dived left, hoping to avoid the strike.

The magic slammed into my leg, making pain tear through my muscles. I shook uncontrollably as I dropped to the ground, tears prickling at my eyes.

"Shit." I clutched my leg, swallowing down bile.

What the hell had he hit me with?

Some kind of crazy electric magic. Cold sweat dripped down my back as I looked toward the demon. He was completely ignoring me, creeping toward the open window.

Bastard thought I was down for the count.

If he'd gotten a more direct hit, I would be.

Whatever he was working with was so powerful—and he was so fast—that my bow and arrow wouldn't do the trick. None of my magic would.

I had to fight fire with fire.

Quickly, I sliced my finger with my sharp thumbnail, smiling slightly at the bite of pain as I called upon my Blood Sorcery. I'd grown to like this pain—it was an indicator that I was in control.

As blood welled, I focused on the demon's signature. It still reeked, but I forced myself to inhale it. It helped me mimic the magic that he'd thrown at me. I'd neutralize him with a bit of his own power. It was one of my favorite tricks. He'd never expect me to throw his own gift at him.

Slowly, it grew inside me, crackling within my chest like electricity. But there was another unfamiliar buzz there. Faint. The magic hesitated, not forming as fast as it normally would.

My Blood Sorcery had been a little uncooperative since I'd gotten my Unseelie wings, but this was worse. The magic inside me was unsettled, no doubt because of my recent transition, but I could still use it. I just had to be careful.

As the demon's electric power surged inside me, I stood. I drew a dagger from the ether, then raised my other hand, aiming for him. I called upon the magic inside me, letting it rise to the surface and flow down my arm.

It shot from me as a bright blue current flecked with

green sparkles, lighting up the night. At the last moment, the demon turned.

He fired his own blast of magic at me, and the two streams met in the middle. I winced, forced backward by the force, but kept my magic flowing. The two streams of electric energy crackled and burned, binding us in a weird dance.

I struggled to keep the magic flowing as I raised my dagger and hurled it at him.

Distracted by our joined magic, the demon wasn't able to dodge the blade as quickly this time. It plunged into his side, and he let out a high-pitched scream, making the hairs on my arms rise.

Our joined magic crackled and danced. The demon's grew brighter, stronger. My breath grew short as I fought it, but something strange happened.

The power that fizzed inside my chest changed. It twisted and writhed.

Oh no. The Unseelie part of me was rising again, sending my own magic out of control. It'd never been this bad, though. This was crazy. True terror fizzed through me, icing my skin and making my stomach turn.

The power burst out of me in a blast. Somehow, it joined with the demon's stronger magic, mutilating itself. Our power fed off each other's, growing brighter and stronger until it exploded in a blast so bright it blinded me.

I flew backward, slamming into the alley wall and sinking to the ground. Pain surged through me as I blinked, my heart thundering in my ears.

All I could see was bright white, then darkness. Magic fizzed in the air. Something was terribly wrong—I could feel it. I scrambled to my feet, my chest feeling hollow and my breath heaving.

I blinked as fast as I could, desperate to see.

Where was the demon?

Was he dead?

My vision returned in blurry bits and snatches. The outlines of buildings appeared first, then the moon. When my sight cleared entirely, I stumbled back, horror chilling me straight through.

In front of me, the ground was gone. The whole street.

In its place, there was an enormous chasm that stretched deep into the earth. I was only alive because I'd been thrown back into the alley when our magic had gone out of control.

The demon on the other side of the street was gone— because the whole earth had disappeared from beneath him. All the way up to the edge of the apartment building.

Fear spiked within me as I inspected the buildings all around. Had I killed anyone?

Please no.

This is what I'd been afraid of. My lack of control over this new magic was causing incredible damage. Maybe death.

None of the buildings had fallen into the great chasm, but it was close. The brick walls had cracked, and glass had shattered as the buildings teetered on the edge of the chasm that stretched fifty feet down the road.

Was it growing?

Magic crackled around my comms charm, and Aeri's voice came out. "Mari? What's wrong?"

"P-problem," I stuttered. "Have a problem."

"Where are you?"

"West side of town." I scanned the street. "What's left of it."

"What do you mean?"

"I destroyed it." Holy fates, my magic had gone so out of control that I'd blasted the town apart.

Dark magic billowed up from the chasm at my feet. Had I opened a portal to the underworld?

I stepped back.

Maybe Tarron had been right to be disgusted by me.

I'd known I wouldn't do anything terrible intentionally. I hadn't planned on *this*.

"I'm coming there now," Aeri said.

"No."

"No?"

"We have to go to the Council. We can't fix this."

"Shit, Mari."

"I know." The Council wouldn't be pleased I'd screwed up like this. They hated cleaning up messes. I'd made a few in my day—particularly when I'd been young and learning the ropes as a Demon Slayer—but *nothing* compared to this. "We don't have a choice."

As if to echo my statement, the earth beneath my feet rumbled, and the crack in the earth opened a little bit wider at each end. Magic's Bend was tearing apart at the seams. For now, it broke apart the street. But soon, the crack would reach the end of the road where more buildings were situated.

When it did, they'd tumble into the earth.

How much more could this thing grow?

I was afraid I knew the answer, and that if I didn't fix this, Magic's Bend could disappear entirely.

"Meet me in the workshop," I said. "We have to report this."

They were the only ones with the resources to help.

"Be there in two."

I gave the great chasm one last look, then used my transport magic to appear back at my house. The old Victorian street in Darklane was just now quieting down for the night. Unlike the west side of town, this neighborhood was hopping through most of the night. The grimy facades of the ornate buildings stared down at me, their blackened windows like eyes. I swore I felt their judgment.

I deserved it.

Quickly, I climbed the stairs to my front door, the Oliver Twistian street lamps shedding a golden glow on the stairs. I let myself into the foyer and hurried back to our workshop.

Normally, the space would calm me. Herbs hung from the ceiling, scenting the air with a spicy, floral aroma, and the shelves were packed full of potion-making tools and books. The hearth lay dark at this hour, barren and cold.

Nothing in the world could calm me now. Normally,

when I was stressed, I'd shove a butterscotch candy into my mouth.

Now was not the time. This was bigger than butterscotch.

Aeri raced into the room behind me, her white bathrobe fluttering around her slender form. Pale blond hair streamed over her shoulders, and her panicked eyes met mine. Whereas I kept mostly nocturnal hours, she'd probably been asleep when she sensed that shit had hit the fan for me.

"How bad is it?" she asked.

"Bad." I stepped toward the table and hovered my hand over one corner.

She mimicked my gesture at the other end of the table, her own magic glowing around her palm. It felt like a cool breeze over my skin and sounded like birdsong. The table lifted itself into the air and drifted to the side wall, then set itself down gently.

Aeri and I approached the trapdoor and sliced our fingertips, each of us letting a drop of blood fall to the stone floor below—black blood for me and white for her. The ground disappeared, a much smaller and more controlled version of what had happened earlier tonight. Still, I couldn't help but shudder as I stepped onto the stone stairs that led deep into the earth.

I led the way, sprinting down the spiral staircase and pausing only to let the protective enchantments make sure that my intentions were pure. When the metal spikes shot out of the wall, I let them take a bit of blood and determine that I wasn't here to do harm. Instead of stabbing me through the sides, they let me pass. On the next level down, the enchanted fog filled my lungs, eventually approving of my intentions. My breath was heaving as I ran into the chamber deep below our house.

The Well of Power glowed blue and bright in the middle of the cavern. It looked like a shallow lake, but it connected us to the Council of Demon Slayers. I yanked off my boots and stepped into the cool liquid. Aeri kicked off her elegant slippers and then followed and grabbed my hand.

"Here we be, let us see," we chanted.

Before we could finish the second verse, Agatha appeared, her ghostly form rising out of the water as gracefully as a nymph.

She never appeared this quickly. It was as if she'd been waiting for us.

"There's a problem," she said. Her features glowed indistinctly with blue light, but I swore I could see concern on her face.

"Yes." My voice nearly cracked.

"Dark magic is seeping into Magic's Bend," she said. "On the west side of town."

"A huge crater has opened in the earth," I said. "It's spreading. It hasn't swallowed any buildings yet, but it will."

"You know about this." Her gaze sharpened.

"I do. And it's bad."

"Give me a moment." She disappeared, and tension tightened my skin.

"Do you think she's checking it out?" Aeri asked.

I gave a tight nod. "Or sending someone else to."

I wasn't sure if Agatha could travel that far from a Well of Power. Her magic was linked to it and all of the other wells. Each Demon Slayer had one in their home, their connection to the Council.

I had to stop myself from crushing Aeri's hand.

A few moments later, Agatha appeared. Her voice sounded stunned. "This is very bad."

I just nodded, my mind racing. I'd caused that. It was *my* fault. Should I confess?

Agatha's gaze zeroed in on me. "It has your magic all over it, Mordaca."

I swallowed hard. Well, that answered that question. "It's my fault. My magic went haywire. I was waiting for an Exurbia demon to show up, like the Council requested. Then another one entirely appeared. I was trying to fight it using his own magic, but something went wrong. Our powers combined, then exploded. And..."

"Opened a hole in the earth," Agatha said. "That is reeking of dark magic."

"Is the darkness escaping into Magic's Bend?" Aeri asked.

"It is, yes. From where, I'm not sure. A dark realm somewhere. The underworld, I think. You said that the demon who showed up wasn't the one our intelligence predicted?"

"Exactly."

She frowned. "Strange. For now, though, the biggest problem is the spreading crater and the dark magic that could spill out."

"How do we stop it?" I asked. "And close it up?"

"You'll need powerful earth magic for that," she said. "More powerful than anything in this realm."

Shit. "What do you mean? Where could it come from, then?"

But as I asked the question, I knew. The knowledge prickled at the back of my mind.

"The Seelie Fae king has the most powerful earth magic that we know of," Agatha said.

Of course he did. Just as I'd expected.

All of the Fae were gifted with natural magics. He could control the elements—one of which was the earth. As the king and most powerful Fae, he'd be the best at it.

Dread expanded within me, filling me up like a balloon that expanded into all my nooks and crannies.

How the hell was this happening?

It was the worst coincidence I could think of.

"You're going to have to ask him for help," Agatha said.

"Um, I'm not so sure that will work." I couldn't meet her gaze.

"Why not? You just helped them defeat the Unseelie Fae incursion into their realm. Surely he owes you a favor."

The Council of Demon Slayers knew almost everything about me. They'd saved me from Grimrealm—the horrible place I'd grown up. They'd given me a job. They knew I was a Dragon Blood, a secret that almost no one on earth knew.

But I hadn't told them about my recent transition to Unseelie Fae. My new wings had vanished almost as soon as they'd appeared, and I hadn't been able to make them come back. And I didn't have any new magic as far as I could tell—just my old magic, suddenly gone haywire due to the changes inside me.

Unseelie Fae were evil, but I wasn't.

That didn't mean I wanted to go around spreading the news of what I'd become.

"We ended things on, ah...iffy terms." As always, it was hard to read Agatha's expression. But it wasn't difficult to feel her surprise that I'd be such a wimp. "But of course I'll go to him and ask for his help. Beg."

Oh fates, this was going to *suck.*

It was the worst thing in the world. Except for Magic's Bend being swallowed by a giant crater or totally enveloped in dark magic.

That was the *actual* worst thing in the world. And I was going to have to beg Tarron for his help fixing my mistake.

I'd rather roll in the vomit that had been next to me in the alley earlier tonight.

"You must go immediately," Agatha said. "We'll cover for you with the Order of the Magica for as long as we can."

"Thank you." The Order of the Magica, along with the Shifter Council, were the two primary magical governments on earth. There were a few smaller ones in other realms—like the Seelie Court of Tarron's and the vampires —but on earth, it was the Order and the Council. The Order oversaw magic users such as myself, and they'd happily chuck me in the Prison for Magical Miscreants if they found out I was a Dragon Blood. If they found out I did this?

Yeah, I'd be in jail.

I shivered.

"And we'll do what we can to slow the destruction of Magic's Bend." Agatha looked at Aeri. "You can help. But we don't have much time."

I nodded, my mind spinning with what was to come. I'd planned to never see Tarron again, despite the fact that we were fated mates. He didn't want to see me, after all.

But now I would.

I had to.

I was going to have to go into his realm and beg for his help.

2

IT HAD ONLY TAKEN AGATHA A FEW MINUTES TO GET ME ONE of the golden medallions that acted as a key to the Seelie Realm. The place was notoriously difficult to get to, but the Council of Demon Slayers had a hookup.

I used those few minutes to freshen up, making sure that my makeup was in place. There was so much black around my eyes that it looked like a mask, and I approved.

Frankly, I looked fantastic.

Which was good, because I *so* did not want to beg Tarron for help. I might as well look like a million bucks while I did it.

I stayed in my black fight wear. There was no question that fixing the crater in the earth was going to be dirty work. Neither the place nor the time for my fabulous dresses.

Once I was ready and Agatha had given me the medallion, I said goodbye to Aeri and transported myself directly to Kilmartin Glen, in Scotland. Storm clouds rolled across the sun, making the green landscape appear ominous. This small bit of Scotland was home to hundreds, probably thousands, of ancient ruins. It was full of Fae magic, and as a result, it was the entry point to their realm, which was sort of on earth, sort of not.

It'd been less than two weeks since I'd come here to compete in the Trials of the Fae as an excuse to spy on Tarron. It felt like a century ago.

I approached the row of standing stones that gleamed with ancient magic. They stood silent and tall, sentries for thousands of years. At the end of the row, I stopped in front of the last stone. It towered above me, twice as tall and three times as wide. Pale green lichen covered the surface, and I placed my medallion into a circular indentation and pressed it inside. Magic sparked, sounding of birdsong and feeling like a warm ray of sun, and a door appeared to my left. It was made of pale, twisted tree limbs. More branches framed the door, covered in white flowers and beautifully decorated.

Everyone was beautiful and fanciful-looking in the Seelie Court. Everyone except their king. He looked beautiful and stark.

I shook away the memory of his face. I'd have to deal with him soon enough, and thinking about him just got my heart rate up.

I retrieved my medallion and turned toward the door, which swung open invitingly. Magical signatures wafted out, all of them earth based. The feel of grass beneath my feet was accompanied by the sound of leaves rustling and the taste of sweet apples.

I stepped through, letting the ether suck me in and spin me through space. It spat me out in a grove of enormous trees, each of them at least four hundred feet tall, with silvery bark and green leaves. It was daytime here, as it was in Scotland. The sun filtered through the trees that towered hundreds of feet above, shooting beams of light that sparkled and danced.

"You're back." The voice that floated toward me was feminine.

I turned, spotting the same guard who'd manned this post when I'd last come here. Her skin was milk pale and her hair a gleaming white. Lavender eyes and pointed ears completed the very Fae look.

I'd never gotten her name before. I stepped toward her. "Yes. I'm Mordaca. And you are?"

"I'm the one who knows just what to do with you." She smiled, and it wasn't pleasant.

A tiny stab of fear pierced my stomach, which annoyed me. I was only afraid in the worst, death-inviting circumstances.

This wasn't it. Surely.

But something about this place—Tarron—put me on edge.

"Do with me?" I asked.

"Indeed." She approached so swiftly that I didn't have a chance to flinch back. Her fingertips landed on my cheek, and hot magic flowed through me.

My eyes rolled back in my head, and I barely felt the ground as I hit it.

The world appeared hazy as my limp body was eventually loaded into a carriage. I was semiconscious, drifting in and out of a haze. I occasionally got a fuzzy glimpse of the pale wooden houses on the outskirts of town. The black cloths still covered the doors, mourning the dead from the Unseelie incursion that had polluted the former king's mind. It had made him kill many of the Fae in his realm. As a result, Tarron had been forced to kill his own brother. He'd tried to save him, but it hadn't worked.

Despite the obvious signs of mourning, the air itself was sweet and pure. The dark magic stench that had pervaded this place last time I was here was fully gone.

Because of me.

Job well done.

I hoped the king remembered that I'd helped him then.

Consciousness faded faster as the carriage rumbled through the castle walls. The ornate structure sat in the center of the town, beautiful and enormous. It was everything that a fairytale castle should be, complete with a monster who lived in the top tower.

I struggled to keep my eyes open as the carriage rumbled around to the back of the building. We skirted around the wall of the castle, and I looked up, my neck limp and my head heavy on the carriage seat below me.

Tarron's tower speared the sky overhead.

Was he in there?

Was that where they were taking me?

It was my last thought before blackness took me.

I woke with a splitting headache and a wide, wet tongue swiping across my cheek.

"Ew!" I scrambled upright, my brains feeling like they'd been mashed.

The thorn wolf sat next to me, huge and weirdly cute. The Fae beast had become my sidekick the last time I was here. He was huge, sitting upright on his butt and towering over me. Instead of fur, his coat was made of thorns. His tongue lolled out of his mouth, making him look like a big goofy dog that could kill you with a few well-placed thorns ejected from his coat.

"Hey, Burn." I reached out and gently patted his head. His full name was Burnthistle, but we'd agreed that was a bit of a mouthful.

Bacon.

It was the only word he knew, and I took it to mean "hello."

"Where am I?"

Bacon.

"The dungeon, huh?" The small space was barren, with huge stone blocks forming the wall and an iron gate that looked impenetrable. "Why the hell would he put me here?"

Bacon.

"Oh, right. It's because I'm an evil Unseelie Fae. The worst of the worst," I joked darkly.

My mind flashed back to the last time I'd seen him—when I'd transitioned to Unseelie Fae. He'd just given me the kiss of a lifetime, and it had somehow jumpstarted the fae energy inside of me. My wings had sprouted from my back, scaring the hell out of me and shocking him. The memory was still fresh in my mind...

Tarron stared at me, anger on his impossibly handsome face. Betrayal flickered in his eyes as they moved from my glittering wings to my face. He looked at me like I was a monster.

"I didn't know what I was," I stammered. "I swear it."

"You didn't know until the wings grew?"

I hesitated, heart pounding. "I knew before then. But only by a few days. When we were in the Unseelie realm, I realized."

He shook his head and stepped away from me, any warmth gone from his face. He didn't care that I was supposed to be his Mograh. *His fated one. But he cared only about the lie he thought I'd told. About his hatred for the Unseelie.*

"You'll never trust me." Hurt tore me apart. He hated the very blood that ran in my veins. "I can see it on your face. Whatever there was between us doesn't matter at all, does it? Not as long as I'm Unseelie Fae."

He nodded sharply. "It's impossible."

"Fine, then." I couldn't take this. He hated my very species. I gave him one last look, and transported away.

I shook the memory away. Annoyance and hurt seethed within me, but I shoved them aside. I really didn't have time for silly things like emotions right now.

I dug into my pocket and drew out a gold foil-wrapped candy. Quickly, I unwrapped it and shoved it into my mouth. It didn't do much to calm me, but it helped.

Burnthistle looked at the gold wrapper with interest, so I dug out one for him, too, and tossed the unwrapped candy into the air. He snagged it and chomped down.

Sucking hard on the candy, I climbed to my feet and inspected the small room. My muscles ached from my fight with the demon earlier, but they loosened up as I moved.

"I'll tell you one thing, Burn. There's no way I'm waiting here for him to call on me." If he ever did. I might be here for years.

Bastard.

The stone walls were solid—not a single secret door to be found—so I turned my attention to the iron grate. There was no one beyond it. No guards or anything down here in the depths of the castle. Just me, rotting away. Magic sparked from the gate, a repelling charm that pricked against my fingertips. When I pressed my hand flat to the lock, it felt like daggers stabbing my palm.

"Ouch." I yanked my hand back.

Did I dare try my magic here? The last thing I needed was a repeat of the chasm that I'd created in Magic's Bend.

But I felt more settled here. Burn pressed himself against my leg, and I felt even better. The magic inside me was calmer. I felt more like myself.

Was it because I was in a Fae realm? Or maybe it was just Burn's help.

Whatever it was, I felt like I could probably control my gifts a bit better. Like I'd been able to before I'd transitioned to part Unseelie Fae.

I had to get out of here though. I was desperate to not be at Tarron's mercy. I'd be begging for his help soon, but I wanted whatever dignity I could muster. Being dragged out of his dungeon for an audience would not start things off on the right foot.

I drew in a careful breath and called upon my magic. It flickered to life inside me, feeling almost normal. Burn helped, his presence calming my magic enough that I could control it. I sliced my fingertip with my thumbnail and called upon my Blood Sorcery. It surged to life inside me, almost too powerful.

Crap. Even here, I still wasn't completely in control.

But I had it mostly, and I kept tight rein on it as I envisioned a new magic—breaking down magical barriers. I'd tear apart the magic that imbued this gate until it was no more. It was something I'd done many times before, and I was familiar with it.

As gently as I could, I pressed my hand to the lock and fed my magic into the gate. Bit by bit, I broke down the protective spell that made touching the gate hurt so much. Finally, it was gone.

The cut on my finger healed, courtesy of a spell that mended that small body part as soon as I wounded it.

Very necessary for a Blood Sorceress.

I reached into the ether for my lock-picking tools and inserted the little metal pins into the lock.

Immediately, they melted, forming a puddle on the ground next to my boot.

I jumped back. "Crap."

Huh. Hadn't seen that spell coming.

I stashed my remaining tools in the ether and sliced my finger again, calling upon a new magic. I imagined melting the metal lock, watching the molten silver drip to the ground. The power surged inside me, and I pressed my hand to the lock.

The entire gate melted, flooding the stone around me with hot, glowing silver.

I leapt backward, heart thundering loudly. "Shit."

Burn blinked at me, turning his gaze between me and the metal.

"Yeah, that was more than I was anticipating," I said.

I had more control of my power in this realm, but definitely not the total control I'd once had.

Damned Unseelie magic. My body didn't know how to handle the newcomer, and this was the result.

"Hopefully Tarron won't check down here for a while." I shrugged. "But then, that's what he gets for locking me in a dungeon."

Burn gave me a look that suggested I was an idiot for being so unconcerned. And maybe I was, since I needed Tarron's help.

"I just won't tell him I melted the gate," I said.

The dog just stared.

I sucked in a slow breath, vowing to be nice to Tarron.

Sweet. To beg prettily for his help. Whatever it took, even though it felt like eating crow.

"Here goes nothing." I gave Burn one last look and jumped over the puddle of molten metal, then hurried through the darkened corridors of the dungeon.

There was no one else down here, but the place didn't feel totally abandoned. They definitely used this sometimes.

It didn't take long to find the stairs that led up to the main part of the castle. Unfortunately, there was a guard standing at the top of them. I could just barely see his shoulder.

I didn't want to fight him up there, and I definitely didn't want to hurt him. That'd be very bad form, indeed. Super rude, considering I wanted Tarron's help.

I drew a dagger from the ether and dropped it to the ground, hoping the clattering noise would draw his attention. I ducked back into the shadows behind the wall as his voice filtered down.

"Who's there?"

I stayed silent, hoping.

Soon, I heard his footsteps. I called on another dagger, this one with a heavy hilt. When he appeared at the base of the stairs—tall and strong and dressed in the red and gold uniform—I leapt out and slammed my dagger's hilt against his head.

He slumped silently to the ground, unconscious. I yanked his braided golden belt off his waist and bound his hands behind his back. Then I tied the laces of his boots together. I didn't need to keep him incapacitated for long, so this should do the trick.

I stood and brushed off my hands. "Not bad."

As quickly and quietly as I could, I raced up the stairs, checking the halls for activity before I slipped out into the main corridor. As with everything in the palace—everything except the dungeons—the hall was huge and airy. Big, glassless windows allowed the breeze to float in, bringing with it the scent of flowers and the sound of birdsong.

It didn't take long to find my way up the stairs toward Tarron's tower. I'd gotten to know the castle a little bit during my last visit. I passed a few of the richly dressed court ladies, their colorful gowns shimmering in the breeze, but they paid me no attention. Apparently Tarron hadn't told everyone I was meant to be tossed into the dungeon immediately upon arrival. Or maybe they just didn't know who I was.

Tarron's tower was the biggest one, located at the highest point of the castle. He kept his quarters separate from the rest, no doubt because he didn't relish being king. I didn't know much about him, but of that, I was certain. Even the court was just for appearances, I was sure, though it was an important part of Fae culture.

Did his people know what their reluctant ruler had sacrificed for them?

He'd had to kill his brother to save them

I couldn't blame him for not relishing the new role that

had been foisted upon him. No matter how ruthless and cold he was, he'd loved his brother.

I reached the main door and didn't bother to knock.

Instead, I pushed it open and stepped into the huge, round tower that acted as his bedroom and main quarters. There was a bed, dresser, and chair in the space, but my gaze went right to him.

He stood in front of the largest window, shirtless and gorgeous.

I almost stutter-stepped backward.

I'd caught him getting dressed. The hard planes of his muscles gleamed in the sunlight, and his dark hair shined like ebony. He was so beautiful that it almost hurt to look at him. He possessed the perfect Fae beauty combined with a masculinity that made my heart race. The power that surrounded him was so strong it was almost scary.

Too bad I liked scary.

And I could *feel* the connection with him.

Fated.

I was his *Mograh.*

And he didn't want me.

Well, I didn't want him.

Green eyes glinted as he sized me up.

I swallowed hard, straightening my spine.

"You." His voice was low and rough.

"Of course, me."

"You broke out."

"Didn't you think I'd try to escape?"

"I had a feeling you might." He shrugged. "But that was quick."

He'd known I would? I hated playing into his hands like that. But then, I hated sitting around in his dungeon more. "Why did you put me there?"

"Why wouldn't I?"

Because I'm your fated mate. Because I thought there was something between us.

I pinched my lips together, unable to speak the words. Whatever closeness there had been was gone. He didn't trust me, and I didn't trust him. Maybe he'd freaked out when he'd learned what I was, but he'd had time to come to me since then.

He hadn't.

It was made worse by the fact that I *was* lying to him. My mother's magical signature had been all over the crystal obelisk that had destroyed his brother and cost the lives of hundreds of his people. I hadn't told him.

Not to protect her. I hated it, but she was obviously evil. I hadn't known how to tell him. And now that I needed his help to save Magic's Bend, I *couldn't* tell him. If he hated me because he thought I'd had something to do with his brother's death, he'd never help me.

And Magic's Bend would be destroyed.

Anyway, whatever we had between us—naturally or ordained by fate—it was dead.

Except my heart didn't believe that. It raced, making my head grow almost faint. I moved my gaze to a spot over his right shoulder.

There was no denying the chemistry that flared between us. I could all but *feel* his desire for me. The fated mate bond made it clear—he wanted me. He didn't want to want me.

But he did.

"Why are you here?" he asked, his tone rough.

Because I want to see you.

My stomach turned at the thought. I hated that it was true. Despite everything, I'd wanted to see him.

I was an idiot. I hated the lack of control I felt over myself around him. This Fated Mate bond thing sucked. I couldn't control my new magic and that was terrifying. I couldn't control my hormones.

Now I had to beg this jerk for help.

This was *so* not my day.

"I need your help." I approached slowly, then stopped a few feet in front of him. "Something terrible has happened in Magic's Bend, and you're the only one with the right kind of magic to fix it."

I made no mention of the albatross between us, but it hung heavy in the air. Despite it, I felt like an invisible force was pushing me toward him.

After a moment, he arched a perfect black brow. "Details?"

He seemed to have no idea what I was talking about, so if he *had* been watching me from the roof earlier tonight, he'd left before the demon had arrived.

I drew in a shuddery breath and explained what had gone wrong in Magic's Bend, leaving out any mention of my role in the issue. He didn't need to know that my Unseelie magic had gone haywire and partially caused it. He hated me because of that very magic. No way I'd mention it now.

"And lives are at risk?" he asked.

"The whole town." Bile rose in my throat at the thought of the damage I'd caused.

I have to fix it.

Even if it killed me.

Which I really hoped it wouldn't.

He frowned. "Why should I help you?"

"I helped you save your realm."

"That's done with, though."

My jaw nearly dropped. "So you wouldn't pay me back by helping me when I need it?"

"It was your job."

"All the same, you benefited."

He shrugged. "Like I said, over and done with."

"I'll never help you again, then."

"Should I ever need it—which I won't—the Council of Demon Slayers will just send someone else."

He was being a bastard just for the sake of it. The animosity sparked between us like a live wire. But at the edges of it, desire flamed. It was a tangible thing between us, impossible to ignore. Whether it was natural or our fated mate bond, I had no idea. But it lit the air up like a wildfire.

The fighting just made it hotter.

I was so pissed at him, but so turned on at the same time.

"What do you want?" I bit out the words, my heart thundering. "I'll do anything."

"Anything?" The heat in his voice made me shiver, and I almost hoped he asked for something that involved touching. A lot of touching. And maybe no clothes.

I'd do it.

I'd be pissed at myself when it was over, but I'd happily jump him and do whatever he wanted me to.

"Anything." My voice was husky.

His eyes turned dark, desire flickering in their depths.

But then he stepped back, shaking his head. The desire faded from his eyes. "Not that."

I shrugged, as if I didn't care.

But I did.

And it stung.

"A favor," he said. "Tell me why the Unseelie tried to invade my realm with their dark magic and evil influences."

"I don't know. I told you that already. I didn't even know I *was* Unseelie."

Skepticism shone in his eyes, and he clearly wasn't ready to believe me. "Then help me figure out why they did it."

"Done." But how the hell was I going to help him with that? I might be part Unseelie, but I didn't even know where their Court was. I knew almost nothing about them, besides the fact that they had wings and their magic was screwing up my own.

That was a problem for future Mari, though.

Right now, I'd do anything it took to close the chasm in Magic's Bend before it destroyed the town.

If I didn't stop that, I'd be as evil as Tarron thought I was.

3

WE DIDN'T SPEAK AS WE MADE OUR WAY OUT OF THE FAE realm and toward the west end of Magic's Bend. When we reached Kilmartin Glen in the human realm, I looked at him.

"Can you transport?" I asked.

"Yes. I can follow your signature and end up near you. But it'll be too dangerous if I'm headed toward a giant pit in the ground."

That was a good point.

And there was only one solution. It made me shiver just to think of it.

I held out my hand. "I'll take us. I know where it's safe."

He looked at my hand, but I couldn't read whatever was in his eyes. When his hard palm met my own, however, I shivered at the heat that raced up my arm. My whole body tingled, and I swore I saw a bit of heat in his eyes.

Memories of our pasts kisses flashed in my mind—him pressed hard against me, his mouth on mine.

I dragged my gaze away and called upon my magic. The ether sucked us in and spun us through space, then spit us out near the west end of Magic's Bend. I'd put us two blocks away from the catastrophe to be safe, but the reek of dark magic stank all the way over here.

Tarron dropped my hand, and I could hear the frown in his voice. "This is bad."

"Wait until you see it." I strode down the street, heading toward the road where the chasm started.

When I reached it, I stifled a gasp. The sun was starting to rise, and it shined on a chasm that was even longer than it had been. People milled around, both locals with horrified expressions and Order members, the government employees who would no doubt try to fix this.

Were any of them looking at me? Did they realize I'd done this?

No, the Council of Demon Slayers was covering for me. Here and there I spotted members of the Council, come to clean up the mess of one of their own.

Fates. This was the *worst.*

Embarrassment heated me, but it was quickly driven out by worry and regret.

I looked at Tarron. "Can you fix it?"

He frowned, his brow furrowed. "You didn't tell me that you caused this."

I swallowed hard. "You can tell?"

"Your signature is all over this." His green gaze

snapped to mine, and his posture shifted, turning warrior-like. "Was it on purpose?"

"No! Of course not. I'd never do this on purpose."

He inspected me, then nodded, almost reluctantly. "I believe that. But what exactly happened?"

I explained about the demon, and how my magic had joined with his and gone haywire. "Probably because of the new Unseelie magic inside of me. I can't control it."

His expression turned skeptical.

"I know you think I've always known that I'm part Unseelie, but I really haven't." I tried to force the truth to shine in my words. "It came as a surprise to me as much as it did to you."

He didn't even nod.

"If I'd known I was Unseelie, I'd have better control over that magic, don't you think?" I asked.

He stared hard at me, clearly trying to decide if he believed me. And hell, we didn't have time for this.

"Will you help me or not?" I demanded, abandoning the attempt to convince him that I hadn't betrayed him and helped the Unseelie invade his realm with their dark magic.

"I'll help you, but now I'm not sure there is much I can do. If it were a normal chasm—not created by dark Unseelie magic—I could knit the earth back together. But there's more to this..."

"What do you mean?"

"You're going to have to help fix it. You're the only one who can undo the magic you've done here. It's like a magnet holding the earth apart. Only once you've removed it can I piece the earth back together."

"Shit. I have no idea how to do that." I shook my head and gestured to the chasm. "I don't even know how I did this."

"You're going to have to get control of your magic, then. It's the only way."

"*How*?"

"Go to the Unseelie Court. Learn where you came from. Only by going to the source of your magic can you learn to control it. There are Fae rituals for these sorts of things."

"I can only learn my magic in the Unseelie realm? I'd really prefer if there were an old book or something."

"That's not really how the Fae do things."

I frowned at him. "You just want to go there to figure out why they invaded your realm."

"I won't lie. That has its appeal."

"Then just go there," I snapped, knowing it was a bit stupid but unable to help myself. Something about him just got my blood pressure up. "You don't need me to go with you on a journey of self-discovery."

"In fact I do. No one knows where the entrance to the Unseelie Court is."

"You can't go through the King's Grove in your realm? The place where the crystal obelisk appeared?" It had linked his realm to the Unseelie one so their magic could flow through.

"No, that's entirely blocked off, ever since we destroyed the obelisk. I don't know how to find the Unseelie."

Shit. I called upon my weak seeker power, knowing it wouldn't work but trying anyway. "I don't how to find them either."

He frowned at me. "Really?"

"*Really.*"

His expression was still skeptical, but I thought that maybe he was finally starting to believe me. "Then we need to find it so that you can fix what you've broken."

My mind raced. He was right. "I think I know someone we can ask."

"Another Unseelie Fae?"

"I don't know any others. I'm talking about three really powerful seekers. Far more powerful than I." Actually, my friends weren't seekers. They were FireSouls—a rare type of supernatural who shared the soul of a dragon. They could find almost anything of value. But since FireSouls were as hunted as Dragon Bloods, they pretended to be seekers.

And I prayed they'd be able to help me, because the only other option was one I *really* didn't like.

Going to Grimrealm to ask my aunt.

Tarron nodded sharply. "We'll go to them now."

I spared the chasm one last glance, hoping that the Order members and the Council could keep the thing under control until I figured out how to get rid of it for good. Then I reached for Tarron's hand.

He gripped mine, and I suppressed a shiver, then let the ether sweep me up and take me home.

We arrived in Darklane as the early morning sun sparkled on the many glass windows of the buildings of Factory row. The three-story factories had all been built in the eighteenth century. After a period of disrepair, they'd been fixed up into one of the trendiest parts of town. Potions & Pastilles was located here, along with Ancient Magic, the shop where the FireSouls ran their business.

"This way." I led us across the street, toward the wide glass window decorated in gold letters that said *Ancient Magic.*

I pushed my way through the door, stepping into an amazing shop filled with magical signatures of every variety. Replica artifacts from ancient historical sites sat on the shelves, each imbued with a powerful magical spell. The three FireSouls—Cass, Nix, and Del—were total bad asses who'd turned their very handy skills at finding treasure into an awesome job.

"This place is impressive," Tarron murmured.

"Right? They're essentially tomb raiders, but ethical about it. Which I didn't even realize was a thing when I'd first met them."

"What do you mean?"

I stepped farther into the shop as I talked. "They work with the permission of the government, hunting down valuable artifacts that were once enchanted by ancient supernaturals. Because magic decays and becomes unstable, they find them before they can explode."

"Ah. They save the whole archaeological site that way, don't they?"

"And sometimes the cities on top of the sites, too."

"Then they sell the artifacts here." He admired a dagger on the shelf to his right.

"Not quite. The artifacts shouldn't be sold to individuals. They're important historical items. Normally they go to a museum, or back to the archaeological site if it hasn't been studied yet. But before that, Nix removes the magic from the artifact and puts it into an exact replica. *That's* what they sell."

"And the artifact can no longer damage the site once it's returned."

"Precisely. Pretty neat system."

"It is."

But there was no one in the shop that I could see. "Hello? Cass?"

"Hang on!" Her voice echoed from the back room, and a moment later she hurried in. Her red hair swung around her pretty face and she was dressed in her usual uniform of trim leather jacket and jeans. She looked exhausted and a bit dirty.

"Mordaca. What's up?"

"Hey, Cass." I gestured to Tarron and introduced him.

"Nice to meet you." He leaned in and shook her hand.

She lingered on his face for a moment longer than normal, clearly assessing him. "That's some serious magic you've got on lockdown, Tarron."

He lifted a shoulder slightly.

Cass was one of the most powerful supernaturals I'd ever met, but right now, she looked wrung out.

"You look like you could use a break," I said.

She leaned against the counter. "Could I ever. But the west end of the city is about to fall into a pit. I've been over there trying to help, but I just came back to check on the shop."

"Yeah, about the crevasse over there..." I met her gaze. "My fault."

"Ohhhh." She made a face. "That's rough."

"Tell me about it. But you didn't realize I'm the cause?"

"No."

The Council of Demon Slayers really was covering my butt.

She frowned. "So what are you doing here if the crevasse is over there?"

"I've just learned I'm an Unseelie Fae and the magic has recently gone haywire inside me. The result is semi-Armageddon."

She squeezed my arm. "It happens to the best of us."

A surprised laugh escaped me.

"How can I help? I'm guessing you need help finding something?"

"Right in one try. I think that I need to find the Unseelie Court in order to master my new magic so that I can fix this."

Her brows rose. "That's a tall order."

"I know."

"Let me see, then." She gestured for my hand, and I

gave it to her, gripping tight. "Imagine how much you want to find it. How much you value it."

Cass could find things because dragons freaking loved treasure. They were geniuses at finding it. If you valued something enough, anything could become treasure.

Even the entrance to the Unseelie Court.

I closed my eyes as her magic welled on the air, imagining how much I wanted to find the court.

I waited, tension gripping me tight. Next to me, Tarron sat stiffly, his gaze intense.

It took her a few moments, but finally, she opened her eyes. "Can you tell me anything about it? Approximate location? What it looks like?"

Shit. Sometimes this happened. I didn't actually value the Unseelie realm—the opposite, in fact. In situations like this, a FireSoul really needed a bit of a clue to go on to help hone their talent.

"It's definitely in Scotland, though we don't know where."

"Hmm." Cass frowned. "That's it?"

"I'm afraid so." I squeezed her hand. "Maybe it'll work?"

"I'll try again."

I waited, breath held.

She opened her eyes. "I need a little more to go on. If you could find a name or a slightly more specific location, I can give you better details."

Double shit. This was what I'd been afraid of.

I withdrew my hand from hers. "We'll work on that."

Dread swelled in my chest, knowing what I had to do next. The only place I could get information about my homeland was from family. And the only family who might know was Aunt, my mother's sister. "But can you do me a favor?"

"Anything."

Gratitude forced out some of the dread. Cass was solid.

"The only place I could possibly get the information is in Grimrealm."

Cass's skin paled. "Mordaca..."

"Yeah, I'm not super pleased about going myself." Not only did I not want to face my past or my aunt, the last time I'd been there had been *hell.* I'd been abducted and held prisoner, while poisoned.

To say the place was full of bad memories was an understatement.

"I'm not going to tell Aeri I'm going. I don't want her to try to come. It's too dangerous. But my aunt..."

"If you're not back in twenty-four hours, I'll come after you."

I loved that she just *got* me. It was a good friendship when your friends instinctively knew you were requesting a possible rescue mission. And going to face my aunt, who'd kept me prisoner for years, definitely might necessitate a rescue mission.

"I'm going with you," Tarron said.

I looked up at him. "Okay."

I wouldn't look help in the mouth—not given where

we were going. And we really should stick together until we got to the Unseelie Court.

I prayed that Aunt would know where it was. I'd never known what kind of supernatural she was supposed to be because she hadn't used magic ever. Aeri and I had theorized that she had none. It was why she'd been so obsessed with forcing Aeri and me to become powerful Dragon Bloods. She'd wanted to use our magic for her own ends.

But maybe she'd been Fae all along. Either she 'd been kicked out of the Unseelie homeland, or she didn't like it there.

I swallowed bile and repressed a shudder.

I had to go back to Grimrealm and face my aunt and uncle.

I'd said I'd do anything to fix what I'd broken, and the universe was cashing in on that.

Cass squeezed my hand. "You'll be fine. You're stronger now."

I nodded, making sure not to meet Tarron's gaze. He didn't know about my past, and I didn't want him to. That horrible part of my life was a secret. I'd felt weak then. Powerless.

I'd never feel like that again. And part of that meant keeping the secret.

"You've been awake far too long," Cass said. "I can see it on your face. Feel it in your magic. You have to rest, if only for a few hours. Then go to Grimrealm and get your answers. If your aunt can't tell you exactly where it is, bring that info back to me and I can probably find it. I just need a bit more to go on."

"I don't have time to rest," I said.

"You don't have a choice, dude. Not only are you tired, but your magic is depleted. I've got a good feel for these things. You need that magic, or you're screwed."

Damn it, she might be right. Magic wasn't infinite. We had to rest to replenish.

"Do we even have time?" I asked. "That chasm is huge."

"It is under control, for now. The Order and Council are working hard on it. I'm headed back there soon."

"Fine." I nodded. "A few hours. Thank you for your help."

"Anytime."

We departed quickly, and as I stepped into the street, exhaustion tugged at me. I was used to a nocturnal schedule, but after being hit by that demon's strange electric magic, I did need to rest. If only for a moment.

"We'll go to my place." I looked at Tarron. "I assume you're coming with me?"

He nodded. "This will work well. While you try to master your magic in the Unseelie Court, I'll try to learn why they invaded us in the first place. And punish them."

"Two birds with one stone. How convenient." If only it weren't my life we were talking about.

He gave me a look that I couldn't interpret, and I shrugged it off and held out my hand. "Want a ride?"

He gripped my palm and I transported us to my street in Darklane.

I led him toward my house, taking the steps two at a time. I disengaged the protective charm on the house and led him to my apartment. He knew all my other secrets, so why not this one? I'd already gotten his blood oath that he wouldn't reveal any information that would hurt me and Aeri, and I wanted to keep an eye on him.

I led him into the cluttered, colorful apartment, wondering how it looked through his eyes. It certainly didn't look like the me that he was familiar with. I knew how I appeared to the outside world—cold, hard, scary, and very fond of black.

This was colorful and warm.

I glanced at him, catching a look of surprise on his face as he took in the living room couch covered in colorful pillows and the painting that was all bright splashes of color. A basket of knitting sat next to the end table, a project I'd been working on for about six years. In all that time, I'd only knitted about ten ugly rows of a scarf.

It wasn't so much that I liked knitting but that I *wanted* to like knitting. So I kept it there, occasionally poking at it but mostly just leaving it sitting. I called it my hobby but it never really went anywhere. I should probably just start collecting antique weapons instead.

"You can sleep on the couch," I said.

"How generous."

"Well, there's only one bed, and I know how you feel about that."

Heat flashed in his eyes, followed by cold.

Yeah, this guy was a trip.

He wanted me—he couldn't help it, I was his fated mate—but he didn't *want* to want me. Not once he'd learned what I was.

But boy, from the look in his eyes, did he *want* me.

I shivered, then forcefully shoved any hot thoughts away.

I never had guests, but I understood the theory of hosting. I should offer him water or the bathroom or something.

Instead, I turned from him and went to the bedroom. Despite the desire that flashed between us, we were primarily a ticking timebomb of animosity and distrust. And hurt. He was cold--driven by his need for vengeance, and he'd do anything to get it. I couldn't trust anything he said when that was his primary motivator. And I was hiding the truth about my mother. He could probably sense that I was lying about something, even if it wasn't what he thought it was.

So yeah, bad combo all around.

Quickly, I stripped out of my fight wear and climbed into bed, wearing just panties and a tank top. It was more than I normally wore, but I wasn't about to sleep naked in the same apartment as Tarron.

Cass had been right, though. I was exhausted.

As soon as my head hit the pillow, sleep crept in at the edges of my mind.

I couldn't help but think about Aeri, who was still busy with the Council of Demon Slayers, trying to keep the chasm from swallowing more of the town. Should I tell her where I was going tomorrow?

No.

I'd be going to confront Aunt.

Normally, we'd have each other's backs no matter what. But I didn't want to put her in that position. She shouldn't have to ever see her again. So I'd sneak away.

Face Grimrealm alone.

It was my last thought before sleep took me and the dreams came. Memories of being locked up in the cellar with Aeri. Without Aeri.

Aunt's face leering through the bars as she commanded me to cut into my veins and create new magic.

We'd risked everything to escape there, smuggled out in barrels by the Council of Demon Slayers. It had been my magic that had allowed us to make contact with them and arrange our escape.

But sometimes, especially in dreams, it felt as if we'd never made it out at all. I was back there in my nightmares, on the cold stone floor in a ragged dress, trying to see through the dark as I dragged a blade across my skin.

"More," Aunt hissed, her pale face gleaming with a demonic light.

"No." It took all my courage to say the words.

"More," she demanded. "Or I'll hurt Aeri."

Fear sliced through me. She'd do it. I knew she would. She'd done it before.

"Don't," I begged.

"Then more."

I dug the knife deeper, letting the blood flow. Aunt wanted me to make a new, permanent magic. The kind that would change my signature forever. Too much of this and the whole world would be able to sense what I was.

I knew what that meant.

Too much of this and I'd be hunted like a dog.

Except, I already lived worse than a dog.

"More!" The light in Aunt's eyes shone brightly. Too brightly. "Two is better than one."

Fear spiked within me.

The lock on the door turned.

"No," I whispered.

The door slammed open, and Aunt stepped through, dragging Aeri.

"No!" I screamed.

And I kept screaming, unable to stop.

4
_____

"Shhhh, shhhh. It's okay."

I jerked awake to the sound of a soothing voice and strong arms wrapped around me. My mind was completely blank for a moment—I had no idea who was talking or where I was—but I knew I felt comfort.

I collapsed against the warm, strong chest of the man who held me, gasping as the memories faded. My mind ran from the nightmares. All I could feel was strong, warm arms wrapped around me.

Protected.

It just felt right, whatever this was. Like our souls were joined.

The room was dark, shadowed. The streetlamps from outside cast a golden slash of light through the room.

My heartbeat slowed, the fear disappearing.

His scent wrapped around me, drawing me deeper. And things changed. Desire flared, impossible to resist. It stirred in Tarron, too. Somehow, I could feel it. The mate bond joined us. My breathing grew short. All I could focus on was the feel of him. His strong arms, broad chest, hot skin.

The world shrunk to just us.

I lifted my head, unable to help myself. There was just enough light to illuminate his face. His eyes met mine. He'd begun to shift, desire turning his eyes dark. Fangs would appear any minute. Maybe even the silver horns that swept back along his skull. A reluctant sounding groan was torn from his throat.

Like he wanted to fight it, but couldn't.

Unable to help himself, his head dipped to mine.

I rose to meet him.

His lips met mine, lush and skilled. He was like a beast uncaged, unable to get enough of me. I clung to him as he ravished my mouth, his strong hands holding me tight to him. He nipped at my lips, then soothed with his tongue.

My head spun as I touched every hard inch of him that I could reach. Shoulders, arms, back. I wanted to yank off my clothes and pull him down on top of me. His hands ran up underneath my shirt, and I shivered.

Yes.

A crack of thunder burst outside, and I jumped, pulling back from Tarron.

Panting, I met his gaze. His jaw was still tight with desire. His now black eyes flashed and his silver horns came out from above his temples and swept back along his skull.

Holy fates, what was I doing?

There were a million reasons this was a bad idea, and I hadn't thought of one of them.

I'd woken from the nightmare, and he'd been here for me. Comforting me.

And it had immediately turned into the hottest kiss of my life.

We couldn't touch each other without it turning into more.

Shaking, I dragged a hand through my hair and tried to get ahold of myself.

"Are you all right?" he asked, concern in his rough voice. Reluctance. As if he didn't want to worry about me, but he did. He felt compelled to take care of me.

I shivered. It was weird, but I liked it.

I just wanted him to *want* to do it.

"Just a dream. No big deal." That dream had been a doozy, tearing me up inside. Probably brought on by my fear of going to Grimrealm. And by the lack of control I felt over my magic. Being in Grimrealm had made me feel out of control, too.

I scooted back on the bed, then leaned against the headboard.

"It seemed like a big deal," he said.

"It wasn't."

He gave me a skeptical look. "Was it about your childhood?"

How was he so insightful? "Maybe. How'd you guess?"

"When you mentioned your aunt earlier, you stiffened."

I shrugged. "She was a bitch." I looked at the clock, realizing that it'd been four hours. Shit. I shoved at him, trying to ignore the firmness of his muscles beneath my hand and how touching him made my heart leap. "Come on. We need to go."

He nodded and stood. Neither of us mentioned the kiss. We'd both lost our minds. But when he left, my gaze lingered on him a little too long as he strode back to the living room.

I scrambled out of bed, determined to get out of here quickly. Not just because Magic's Bend needed saving from my screwup, but because I didn't want to run into Aeri and tell her where I was going. She'd probably be checking in any moment, and I needed to be well on my way.

I raced into the shower and scrubbed up in three minutes flat. It wasn't a great job, but I was mostly clean and my makeup was all gone. When I climbed out, I went to the mirror and stared into the steamy surface.

My disguise was gone.

I'd stay like this, since I was going to face Aunt.

No way she'd get to see my Mordaca look. It had started as a disguise meant to hide me from her if she ever left Grimrealm—and it still was, to some extent—but it was also *me*. It was the me I'd created from the ashes of my old life—a scary, stone-cold bitch who lived life as she pleased.

I was still that person without the makeup and hair,

but I didn't want Aunt seeing that part of me. It was mine. I'd gone to Grimrealm in that disguise earlier this year, but then, I'd been intending to hide from Aunt while I was there, not seek her out.

Now, I'd be going right into the lion's den. I wanted to be able to return to earth and put it all on and know that it was still mine. That she'd never see it.

So, barefaced it was. I slicked my hair back in a simple ponytail and put on my black leather fight wear. While standing in front of the mirror, I did a simple glamour to make it bright red.

I pursed my lips and tilted my head.

Hmmmm. Still a bit boring.

So I made my hair red, too, using the same glamour spell. It was a brilliant fire engine color to match the suit. I had a friend in Edinburgh who dressed like this—Melusine—and I liked the look.

Ready to go, I went to the living room.

Tarron was dressed, and he turned to face me. His eyes widened. "That's a change."

"It was time for one."

"It doesn't have anything to do with the fact that you're going to face your aunt?"

I shrugged, not liking how close to the truth he was getting, then went to the kitchen. I popped a butterscotch hard candy into my mouth as I walked. "We need food."

He followed me, and I rummaged through the fridge, finding two cold bacon sandwiches. Leftovers from takeout yesterday. As far as I was concerned, bacon was the perfect food, even if it was cold. I had that in common with Burn.

I handed Tarron one, then strode toward the door. "We can drive to the entrance to Grimrealm. I'd like to save the magic instead of transporting."

"It's not far?"

"It's too close, in fact." I chomped on the sandwich as I went to my workshop and found two potions that would make our magic reek as if we were evil, along with a powerful truth serum. Last, I grabbed two long black cloaks from the closet. I swallowed the last bite of sandwich and handed him a small vial of blue liquid that would make him stink like a true Grimrealmer. "We're going to Grimrealm, where only the evilest supernaturals live. Your magical signature will make you stand out like a sore thumb"—it didn't smell or feel *nearly* bad enough —"so drink that to make you blend in. And wear the cloak if you like. Most people do, down there."

"No one wants to be known, then?"

"Nope. Not even to each other. The Order of the Magica doesn't do much down there, but they know it exists. They could toss those folks in jail for all number of dark magic crimes if they really wanted."

I uncorked the vial. I had a very slight dark magic signature myself—a bit fishy, but nothing terrible—which was a legacy of my upbringing in Grimrealm. It wasn't enough to allow me to pass as a local down there.

I swigged down the potion in the vial, gagging slightly

at the sour taste, then shivered as I felt the magic change inside me.

I smelled of *very* rotten fish and a dumpster full of old gym socks. Tarron wasn't much better.

He grimaced. "I don't see how they live like this."

I shrugged, then swirled the cloak on. "I don't want to know."

He draped the black cloak over his shoulders, and I led him out of the house and to the side alley where I stored my baby—a Mustang Shelby GT500, complete with a super loud engine and a glittering black paint job. It'd been enchanted to only turn on at my touch, and I climbed inside and made the magic happen. It roared to life.

Tarron slid into the passenger seat. "This is quite the vehicle."

"A bit different than the carriages in your realm." I winked and pulled out onto the street. I quite liked the carriages, actually. But I'd always like my baby the best.

I drove us through Magic's Bend, heading toward the Historic District where the entrance to Grimrealm was located. It was far too close to Darklane for my comfort.

To distract myself, I asked, "Do you come to earth often?"

He nodded. "As often as I can."

"Not satisfied in your Court?"

He hesitated, and I glanced over, spotting indecision on his face.

"What is it?" I asked.

"I never wanted to be king." The words were stiff, but I could hear pain at the edges.

"Because you loved your brother." It was easy to forget that about him when I was busy being pissed that he hated my species. The Unseelie had done worse than kill his brother. They'd created the circumstances where Tarron's efforts to save his brother had actually killed him.

"Because I loved my brother, and that was his role." He nodded. "He was a good king, until the Unseelie Fae sent their magic to my realm and polluted his mind."

I nodded, my heart hurting for all he'd gone through. If that had been me and Aeri, I'd be a puddle of goo on the ground, never able to move again.

Man, we both had our messed-up pasts.

I pulled into a parking space in the Historic District, a part of town that looked a lot like Darklane, except without the dark magic soot. The buildings were all ornate Victorian structures painted many different colors, with carved wood detailing and charming names over the shops, restaurants, and bars. It was late afternoon, so there weren't many parking spots available, but I got lucky. I climbed out of the car, and Tarron followed.

"This way." I felt his gaze on my back as I strode toward the alley that led toward Grimrealm. As we approached, a miserable, prickling magic spiked my skin, and I got a nearly overwhelming urge to turn back.

It'd work on anyone who didn't know that they wanted to reach Grimrealm.

"That's some protective charm," Tarron muttered.

"Seriously." I pushed through, entering a spotlessly clean alley. Unlike the other ones in this part of town—which was known for its great restaurants and bars—it didn't reek of pee. None of the drunken partiers bothered to push through the protective charm.

"It's in here?" Tarron sounded skeptical as he took in the entirely empty alley with a brick wall at the end.

"Just keep going." I reached the dead-end and pressed my hand to the brick surface. It felt rough—like any normal brick. But I kept pushing, until my hand sank through the stone. It felt like pushing my way through viscous goo. I added my foot, pressing so hard that I it sank into the stone.

Tarron joined me, and we forced our way through into an identical, perfectly clean alley.

"Not what I was expecting," Tarron said.

"They're serious about hiding." I approached the far end of the narrow corridor, which was identical to the one we'd just walked through. When I reached it, I turned to look at Tarron, then pointed to the wall to my left. "Stand there, please."

He did, crossing his arms over his chest and waiting. In his dark cloak, with his midnight hair, he looked like some kind of warrior knight Fae. I hated to say that I liked the look.

Annoyed with myself, I turned back to the wall and studied the bricks there, dredging up my memory of Aeri pressing them in a particular order. It took two tries, but I managed. I could feel it when it worked, magic popping on the air.

I turned and looked at the patch of ground between me and Tarron. It opened up to reveal a pit, and dark magic billowed out, bringing with it the stench of rotten eggs and sewage.

I walked toward it, then met Tarron's eyes. "Here goes nothing."

I jumped into the hole, knowing he would follow. For a moment, wind tore at my hair and my stomach pitched. Then magic slowed my descent, and I landed in an underground tunnel with a pressed dirt floor. Green flame torches lined the walls all the way down. I stepped toward them, moving aside so Tarron wouldn't land on me.

He appeared next to me, in a fighting stance with eyes wary.

Fortunately for us, there was no one here.

Unfortunately, the magic that protected the tunnel had probably changed since last time I was here.

I moved toward Tarron, holding up my hand so he wouldn't walk any farther into the tunnel. "This leads to Grimrealm. It's also one of the few places that we can use to transport out."

"It's impossible to transport from within Grimrealm?"

I nodded sharply. "It's magically banned. There are only a few places within that will allow transporting to the outside world, and I don't know where they are."

"So it'll be a long run back here if we get in trouble."

"Exactly." I pointed to the tunnel. "At the end of this is

the main market and the rest of Grimrealm. There will be protections on it, though. Last time, it was icicles that shot from the walls. Before that, flames."

"Now?"

"No idea." I drew a dagger from the ether, along with a shield. "But I like to be prepared."

Tarron did the same, opting for a sword and shield.

Good choice. I could handle long-range, he could deal with short. My skin chilled as I crept through the tunnel, waiting for the attack.

When it came, it shot from the ground.

"Look out!" I hissed.

A root rose up and twisted around my ankle. I flinched, then reached down and swiped at it, severing the woody stalk so it fell away. Another stretched from the wall, headed for my arm. I lunged, but it was fast, wrapping around my bicep. My heart thundered. It squeezed tight, and I nearly dropped the dagger I clutched in that hand. I stashed my shield in the ether and grabbed the dagger with my free hand, then sawed at the root.

Tarron wasn't faring much better—roots had twined around his ankles and one arm.

But instead of fighting them, he frowned with annoyance.

I hacked at mine, demanding, "Why aren't you doing anything?"

"I am."

His magic began to glow around him, the green aura growing brighter. The sound of wind whistling through the trees grew, and I felt the caress of the ocean against my skin. The scent of an autumn day fought back the stench of the tunnel.

As his magic flared, the roots weakened. They withered and fell away from my arms and legs. The stalks that had wrapped so tightly around me retreated into the earth. Then the same happened to him.

Ah, of course.

"Earth magic," I said. "They didn't count on a Fae coming down here."

"They don't count on many coming down here, it seems."

"No. Only the regulars."

With the vines retreated back into the earth, we were able to hurry through the tunnel toward the far end. The refreshing scent of Tarron's magic faded, and the reek of dark magic surged in to fill its place. I breathed shallowly through my mouth, trying not to smell it.

As we neared the end of the tunnel, I flicked up my hood and tried to ignore my racing heart.

"Mari? Where are you?" Aeri's voice filtered from my comms charm.

Crap. I touched it to ignite the magic within. "I'm hunting a lead. Where are you?"

"At the chasm, helping the Order of the Magica and the Council of Demon Slayers control the chasm. It's growing."

I flinched. "How bad?"

"More than halfway to the end of the street. A lot more."

She didn't say that when it reached the end of the street, those buildings would fall in and Magic's Bend would start to disappear. She didn't need to.

"The dark magic is growing as well," she said. "The Council thinks that eventually, demons could pour out into Magic's Bend."

"So it really is some kind of portal."

"Probably to the original demon's underworld, yes. The one whose magic combined with yours to create the chasm."

Oh, fates. I'd screwed up so bad. "I'm on a lead. I can fix it, Aeri. I just need a little time."

"I'll give you as long as I can. But where are you?"

"Gotta go, sorry." I cut communication.

"You really didn't know you were Unseelie Fae?" Tarron asked.

I looked at him, shocked. "*Now* you want to talk about that?" I pointed to the end of the tunnel, which was only fifty feet away. "We're almost there."

He shrugged. "It was something your sister said. About the chasm growing wider. It doesn't make sense that you would intentionally harm your own town."

"Duh." I glared at him. "It doesn't make sense that I'd hurt yours either. Especially when I risked my life in those Trials in order to *save* it."

He nodded sharply. "I'm beginning to see that."

"Stubborn man." I shook my head and approached the end of the tunnel, trying to ignore the slight flare of hope that he was beginning to believe me. I was still pissed he hadn't believed me in the first place.

It was logical to assume that pain and anger over his brother's death had clouded his judgment, but it was still painful to be on the end of his mistrust.

Even if I sort of deserved it.

He mistrusted me about the wrong things. But all the same, he was right not to trust me.

And I hated it.

Not important.

Not right now. Not when I was walking into my past. Into the past that had hurt me so badly. There could be no soft spots on me right now. I would tell him the truth eventually, but now was not the time.

I reached the end of the tunnel and paused, unable to help myself. The central market spread out before me, the same as it had ever been. This massive domed space deep beneath the earth was the heart of Grimrealm. Here, supernaturals traded in all sorts of dark magic, operating out of the black fabric tents that filled the space to bursting.

Hundreds of people milled between the stalls, inspecting the wares. Everything from potions to shrunken heads and enchanted weapons filled the space. Seers and fortune tellers and mercenaries picked up clients here, along with other unsavory sorts that practiced magic I'd only ever heard of.

And coming from me, that was saying something.

"The magical government just lets this place exist?" Tarron asked. "It reeks of evil."

I nodded shortly. "My friend Claire is a mercenary for the Order of the Magica. Occasionally she works down here. Apparently, they think it's better to have this place exist and use it to catch the baddest of the bad. I'm not sure they aren't a little bit corrupt, though."

"My money's on that option."

"Agreed." I drew in a deep breath and reached for Tarron's hand. "Come on."

5

I GRIPPED HIS STRONG PALM IN MY SMALLER ONE AND TUGGED him through the market. He hesitated briefly, as if surprised I'd touch him, but I just pulled harder. It was so crowded here that I didn't want to get separated. Not to mention, some of these stall operators had magic that could compel you to stay and look at their stuff. I'd learned that last time I was here, and I didn't want to fall prey to it.

Tarron followed close behind me as we wove our way through the stalls of people shouting about their wares. At one point, a woman grabbed Tarron's arm to stop him so he would look at her collection of dried, severed demon hands. I could feel her magic wafting toward him, trying to make him linger and buy one of her gross offerings.

I tugged at him and glared at her. "Back off."

She raised her hands. "Okay, honey. I won't mess with your man."

I scowled at her, then turned and continued through

the market. At one point, a skinny demon grabbed my shoulder to convince me to peruse his collection of stolen charms—they had to be stolen; demons weren't great charm makers—and Tarron pulled me along.

Finally, we made it through the market to the far end. Now that we were away from the influence of the stall owners, I dropped Tarron's hand. Here at the edges of the market, the walls of the great domed space had been carved out to house the larger shops and casinos. This was where the real money was made, and the worst magic went down. Each place was guarded by a bruiser of a bouncer. All of them had magic, and I was glad I wasn't trying to get past any of them.

"Where are we headed?" Tarron asked.

"The poorer neighborhoods are back here." I pointed to one of the many tunnels that extended off the main part of the market. "Each tunnel is like a neighborhood, with apartments built into the stone walls. We lived down this one."

"Do you know if your aunt is still there?"

"No idea. Probably."

"Lead the way."

Tension tightened my muscles as I headed toward the tunnel that had once been our street, stopping in front of the sign on the wall. *Arition Street.* I shivered and tucked myself into a dark corner, dredging up my courage.

Tarron followed me into the shadows, his presence a comfort and a distraction. He stood so close that I could feel the heat of him, and I tried to focus on that instead of my fear.

"I vowed never to come back here," I muttered, pissed that I'd gotten myself into this situation.

"You didn't have to," Tarron said.

I shot him an annoyed look. "My alternative is letting my town fall into a pit of black magic, so yeah, I had to."

"You could have tried to master your Fae magic and never caused the problem in the first place."

"I did!" I seethed with annoyance, and I turned to look up at him. "I've tried to make those damned wings appear a hundred times. I spent all week trying. And the magic inside me? That's a freaking mystery. I have no idea how to control that."

He frowned. "Really? None at all?"

"No. It's a magic that has existed inside me forever, apparently, but it's been dormant. Going to the Unseelie realm to destroy the Obelisk woke it, but I have no experience with it. Honestly, I had no idea it was so dangerous."

He looked torn, his brow creased and his eyes dark. "I'll help you."

"You'll what?"

"I'll help you master your Fae magic. You have to go to the Unseelie Court to start the process of gaining control of it, but I'm certain that's not all of it. You'll have to practice. And I'll help you."

"Why? I thought you hated me." *Despite the fact that I'm your fated mate.*

That was the part that burned the worst.

"Hate you?" The words sounded torn from him. He gripped my shoulders, looming over me. "Never. No matter how much I might want to."

"You *want* to hate me?"

"No." Again, the words sounded torn from him. He was so close that I could feel the conflict inside him. Feel the struggle. "When I thought that you'd been part of the Unseelie Fae incursion that had led to my brother's death, I wanted to. But I couldn't."

"Because of the fated mate bond."

"Yes, because you're my *Mograh*. And also because I've grown to know you better. I know you wouldn't do that."

"Good."

"I'm not sure I'll ever trust you, but I could never hate you." The tension around us tightened, cocooning us in a bubble, away from this horrible place. In the quiet shadows where we stood, his face was the only thing I could see. His green eyes were riveted to mine.

He was probably only helping me so that he could get revenge for his brother. I couldn't really believe that he had feelings for me. Especially since the fated mate bond was probably driving them.

But I couldn't help how I felt. I wanted him. The lack of control drove me crazy. Scared me, even. Because one day he'd find out about my mother, and he'd know he was right not to trust me.

He wouldn't care that I'd done it for Magic's Bend.

But there was no fighting it. Not now. He pulled me

toward him, his gaze dropping to my lips. My heart raced, and I lifted my hands toward his waist.

Kiss me.

Then he shuddered. "No. We're in Grimrealm."

He released me and pulled back.

The tension was broken.

Cold air rushed over me.

He was right.

Somehow, he'd made me forget this place.

That could get me killed.

I sucked in a deep breath and turned from him, giving him one last glance. Whatever was between us wasn't withering away.

Far from it.

Despite the mistrust and circumstances, it was still growing.

But now was *definitely* not the time.

I started down the narrow tunnel. I hadn't been to this place in years, and it looked different. Not smaller, but quieter. Almost dead. Doors dotted the tunnel every thirty feet. Most were shut, but no light shined through the gap at the bottom. A few hung open, silent and empty.

I shivered.

"This place feels abandoned," Tarron said.

"Maybe it is." What if Aunt wasn't here?

No.

As much as I didn't want to see her, I had to.

I'd find her.

We neared the end, where our apartment had been

located. Not that Aeri and I had ever really lived in the main house.

My skin turned to ice as I approached the closed door. Not only was it silent, it *felt* silent. Dead.

I didn't bother to knock, and I didn't hesitate. I just reached for the knob and turned.

It opened easily. "Huh. I'd been prepared to kick it down."

"I think you wanted to kick it down."

"Kinda did." I peered into the darkened interior, heart thundering.

Was Aunt waiting? Lurking?

Where was Uncle?

But no one was there. The place was totally empty. The big main room that housed the kitchen and the living room was nearly stripped of furniture. Dust gathered in the corners, and the air smelled stale.

I charged in, striding toward the back hall where Aunt and Uncle's bedroom had been located.

There was nothing.

Not even a bed or nightstand.

I frowned, cold dread slicking my skin.

As I checked the other three empty rooms, it only grew worse.

"They aren't here."

"What about this trapdoor?" Tarron pointed to the wooden door in the floor that I had avoided looking at when I'd walked into the small room.

"They wouldn't be down there."

"Are you sure?"

"Yes," I snapped. "Because that's where they kept us."

His eyes darkened as understanding dawned.

Shit.

I shouldn't have said anything. Shouldn't have mentioned it.

"They kept you in the dungeon?"

"Why do you think I didn't want to come here?"

"Why did they keep you there?"

"I don't want to talk about it."

"I do."

"Too bad."

He frowned, but took the hint and didn't ask any more. Instead, he turned to the trapdoor and opened it.

I reached out my hand to stop him, but bit back the word, "Don't!"

I couldn't wimp out here. No matter how much I didn't want to go back to that place.

What if there was a clue about Aunt down there?

Dust wafted up as the trapdoor opened, and Tarron laid it on the stone. Then he climbed down into the pit that was the scene of all my nightmares.

I followed, almost in a trance. As I climbed down the stairs to the cold dark dungeon below, my head buzzed and my skin chilled.

The corridor in the dungeon was narrow and tight. There were four rooms—two off of each side.

The familiar scent nearly made me retch. My breath grew shallow.

I followed Tarron as he peered into each room, pulling myself back from the brink.

I was an adult.

I was a stone-cold bitch.

If Aunt appeared here right now, I'd tear the information out of her and then kill her while smiling into her face and memorizing her screams.

There.

That made me feel a bit better.

Tarron turned to me, taking in my no-doubt pale complexion. My pupils had to be as big as saucers, and I wasn't exactly sweating gracefully.

He frowned. "I won't let anything happen to you, you know."

"Thanks, but I take care of myself."

But despite my snappy words, I appreciated it. And hell, I was no dummy. Tarron was strong as hell, with seriously powerful magic.

I was glad he was on my side. If it came down to him saving me or my pride getting me killed or recaptured, I'd sure as hell let him save me.

I drew in a deep breath and finished the search, determined to put this place behind me. There were no clues in the horrible little rooms, just cold and misery. I wished I could say that I put my demons to rest on that visit, but it'd be a lie.

I climbed out of the dungeon first, noticing that Tarron lingered by the stairs to let me go ahead of him. He didn't say he knew I wouldn't like being alone down there; he just acted on it. Which I appreciated even more.

Once he'd made it up through the trapdoor behind me, I stepped around him and spit into the dark hole. "Fuck you."

"I think we can do better than that." He raised his hands, and his magic flared.

I stared at him, confused.

Then the earth rumbled below my feet, and I nearly jumped. I looked down into the dark hole, unable to see anything but the stairs at first. Then earth rose up, rocks and rubble pushing up from deep in the earth, filling in the dungeon so it no longer existed.

Warmth filled me like a balloon, so much of it that I thought I might burst or float away.

It was literally the most thoughtful present that anyone had ever given me.

Tears pricked my eyes, and I blinked, shocked.

I wasn't a crier.

But damned if I wasn't touched.

"What do you say we do the whole place?" Tarron asked.

I just nodded dumbly, then walked out of the apartment backward, keeping my eyes on the piles of rock that belched out of the tunnel, filling the room. He was bringing the earth up from down below in order to not damage the structural integrity of the tunnels.

I stepped out into the main street, where the tunnel was taller and wider. It didn't take long for Tarron to fill the entire apartment with rubble. He brought so much up from deep in the earth that it filled the place until it was entirely gone. Just a wall of rock.

Then he lowered his hands, and his magic faded.

"Thank you." I couldn't look away from him.

He just nodded, then looked toward the street. "Where to next?"

I tried to shake off the emotions that surged through me and focus on the task. "We need to do some recon."

I tried my seeker sense, but was unsurprised to find my aunt's location blocked. The paranoid bitch would have definitely bought a charm to protect against that kind of thing. She'd had a lot of enemies.

I spotted a figure at the far end of the street. Slender and small, his form didn't look familiar.

Tarron noticed my gaze. "Who is that?"

"No idea." I raced toward him, calling upon my unnatural speed that was a gift of my Dragon Blood side.

The stranger flinched and began to run, but I was too fast. When I appeared next to him and grabbed him by the arm, I realized that I'd been right. Totally unfamiliar. But he was definitely interested in what was going on near my aunt's place. His pale green gaze moved between it and me.

His hair was limp and greasy, and the scent of burning garbage wafted from him. "Who are you?"

"None of your business." I drew a dagger from the ether and slammed him back against the stone wall. "Who are you?"

"None of your—"

I pushed my arm against his throat and cut off his words. "You're going to answer me, or I'm going to gut you."

He paled, probably because he could sense that I meant it. I probably wouldn't kill him, but I'd definitely hurt him to get the information I needed. The scent of his magic made it clear what he got up to in his spare time. You could hide a lot of things behind clever words and the right persona—but you couldn't hide evil deeds from reeking through your magic.

"What do you want to know?" he squeaked.

"The man and woman who lived in the apartment we just destroyed—where are they?"

"Dead?"

"Dead?" I hissed.

"Uh, just the man."

Uncle was dead.

Good.

"And the woman?"

"She moved to the forest."

"Which forest?"

He frowned, clearly perplexed that I didn't know. I shook him.

"The one at the end of Midnight Lane, next to the cemetery."

"Why'd she go there?"

"Had to. She had a run-in with a witch who didn't like her. The man died, but she was punished. She moved to the forest."

"Punished how?" I didn't hate the sound of that, to be honest.

"I don't know." He raised his hands. "I swear it. I just heard the rumors."

"Did the witch clear out this whole street?" I asked.

He nodded. "Her magic left a stain here. No one wanted to stay."

That explained the dead feeling to the place.

"How do I find the woman?"

"Just follow the path. There's only one house in the whole forest." He shuddered. "Place is awful."

If it was too terrible for even a Grimrealm local, then yeah, it would be horrible.

I dropped him, then stepped back. He scuttled away so fast that he was out of sight in seconds.

I turned to Tarron. "Looks like we're headed to the forest."

He nodded. "Do you know where the cemetery is?"

"I do." I led the way out of the tunnel, and we cut across the edge of the market, heading for another passage off the bustling space.

We passed two casinos and a shop with totally blacked-out windows. It reeked so badly my eyes watered, and I had absolutely zero desire to see what was inside. Finally, we turned down Midnight Lane.

Unlike Arition Street, there were no doorways leading off this passage. It was empty and quiet, the domed ceiling looming high overhead. As we neared the forest, the sound of night creatures grew louder. Crickets and bats.

We reached the end of the tunnel and stared out into a massive space filled with a forest. We had to be underground still—there'd been no elevation change—but the ceiling was so high above and it was so dark that I couldn't see where it ended.

I could see the shadows of trees, however, and there were hundreds. They were enormous, with black bark and dark gray leaves.

"How is this possible?" Tarron asked. "There's no sun down here for a forest."

"Maybe they don't live off sunlight." I peered at the trees, trying to figure them out. "Because they don't look like any trees I've ever seen."

"No, they look dead." He approached the closest one and pressed his hand to the bark. "And yet, they are not."

"The path is there." I pointed to the narrow, well-trodden pathway. It was so dark that I could only see a few feet down the path, but it was distinct.

"I could create some light, but I'm not certain we want to draw attention to ourselves."

"Agreed." I stepped onto the path.

As soon as I did, lightning bugs lit up the night around me. Hundreds of them, glowing golden and bright. Enough that I could see the woods around me.

"It seems there's no need," Tarron said.

I smiled, almost liking the lightning bugs. Not everything in Grimrealm was bad. We'd come from here, after all. So had Aeri's hellcat, Wally. He was pretty cool.

Quickly, I made my way down the path, my heart beating louder and louder.

Tarron stayed close behind me, and I was glad he was there. As glad as I was that Aeri wasn't.

The forest bustled with life, all of it slightly different than the life on earth. Whatever was feeding this midnight forest, it was doing a good job.

Sounds rustled in the trees around us, and I stiffened. "Do you hear that?"

"I do. Something is watching us."

I wanted to draw a weapon from the ether, but that could signal aggression. There was no need to start a fight if we didn't have to.

I kept my pace steady as I walked, searching the forest around me. The hordes of lightning bugs cast a golden glow, but whatever watched us hid in the shadows.

When the first projectile hurtled toward me, I sensed it more than saw it. I dived left, barely avoiding the narrow dart that whizzed by.

"Shields!" Tarron drew his from the ether.

I yanked mine out as well, crouching behind it as I surveyed the terrain around us.

I saw nothing.

"Quick little bastards," I muttered.

"How do you know they're little?"

"I think the dart flew from low to the ground."

As if to prove my point, a tiny figure sprinted toward us from out of the woods, a narrow pipe raised to his mouth. His skin was blue and his eyes tiny. Spikey green twigs decorated his head, and he moved in a dancing sort of way, with great leaps and hops. He shot a dart right at me, then sprinted behind a tree trunk.

I raised the shield so the dart plonked off the surface, then looked at Tarron, who hid behind his own shield. "They have darts. Probably poisonous."

He nodded sharply.

More of the darts banged against my shield. I peeked out at the forest and spotted a half dozen of the little creatures darting between the trees, shooting at us.

"Let's go side to side," Tarron said. "We'll hold our shields behind us."

"Behind?"

"I'll send a blast of wind out front."

"Perfect." I stood, shifting to stand nearer to him, and we blocked the space behind us with the shields.

His magic flared to life a millisecond later, a strong wind blowing in front of us. Every little creature that tried to shoot a dart saw his weapon lost to the wind.

When they began to move around to the side, I drew a dagger from the ether and hurled it. I sliced one beast through the arm, and it howled. Then another through the leg, and it limped away.

But there were so many of them. Even with Tarron's strong gale deflecting the darts, they could sneak around from the back and maybe get our ankles beneath our shield.

The thorn wolf appeared a moment later.

"Burn!"

He woofed at me, then lowered his head and growled at the tiny monsters who surrounded us. They blew their darts toward him, but the little projectiles bounced off his thick coat of thorns. Burn growled and shot several thorns from his coat, which pierced the monsters straight through.

They shrieked and ran, and we were able to pick up the pace. Tarron never dropped control of the gale that kept us safe from the front, and Burn guarded our backs and Tarron's side. I took care of my side, hitting another little monster with a dagger to the chest.

By the time the tiny creatures had disappeared, I was out of breath.

"Is that all of them?" Tarron asked.

"I think so. The forest seems quieter." Except for a malevolent feeling coming from up ahead.

But I had a feeling I knew what that was.

"My aunt. I think she's near."

We crept forward on silent feet, following the path with Burn at our side. He sniffed the ground occasionally, growling low in his throat at whatever he sensed.

When we came across the house in the middle of the clearing, I stopped, staring.

It was made of bones.

6

"I THOUGHT YOUR CHILDHOOD HOME WAS BAD," TARRON said. "But this is...a fairytale nightmare."

I nodded, taking in the thousands of bones that had been used to build the large round structure. The house was domed, created of bones piled up. Spiderwebs extended up from it, thousands of meters of it creating a white net around the place and up into the huge trees that loomed around. They were hundreds of feet tall here.

I'd never thought I'd say that the dungeon Aunt had kept us in was better than anything.

But it was better than this.

I sucked in a deep breath. "The man on Arition Street said there was only one place in the woods, so this has to be it."

And somehow, I could feel her here. Not her magic, since she didn't really have any of that. But the absence of a soul, almost.

I wouldn't be surprised if she didn't have a soul.

I started forward, my footsteps light on the ground so my approach was silent.

Tarron joined me, staying close to my side. I didn't mean to, but I couldn't help but draw energy from him. Support.

Whether or not he intended to comfort me, I didn't know. But I wouldn't dwell on it.

When I reached the wide front door—once again, made of bones—I stopped and drew in a deep breath. Then I pushed it open. There was no doorknob and no lock, which was odd enough, but the sight inside made me stiffen.

A massive spider crouched against the far wall, staring at me. Glittering, multifaceted eyes met mine, and the huge body was hairy and ugly. A strange nest was built into the corner, and the bones of dead animals lay scattered all around.

Next to me, Tarron drew his sword from the ether.

I couldn't.

Shock rooted me to the ground.

This was my aunt. I could feel it. Could see it in her eyes.

"You look different." I ran my gaze over her horrifying body. "Almost an improvement, really."

The spider hissed, but when it spoke, it was with my aunt's voice. "What are you doing here?"

I shrugged. "Came to pay a visit to family. We were so close, after all."

She hissed again.

"Is Uncle really dead?" I asked.

"Dead as a doornail."

"Or dead as your soul." I felt nothing but seething satisfaction.

Would I kill her?

Maybe.

"How did this"—I gestured to her form—"happen?" I tried to make my voice sound sympathetic so she would tell me, but she could probably see right through it. I wanted all the gory details, my aunt's misery spelled out in front of me.

Apparently I was a bit vindictive.

Who knew?

The spider tapped its front leg against the ground, an almost impatient gesture. Or worried?

When the words came out, it was as if she were desperate to talk. The energy between us was weird as hell, but that didn't stop her. "Our bodyguard was killed two months ago. When that happened, the witchy creditor came for us. She killed your uncle and turned me into this...thing."

The disgust in her voice was evident, and I tried not to smile widely. Not just because she was getting her just deserts, but because Aeri and I had killed that bodyguard. Aeri had delivered the final blow. She'd love to hear the results of her handiwork.

"And you've been alone here since?" I asked.

"The people of Grimrealm evicted me."

"Ooh, rough." I winced. She was too horrible for even the people of Grimrealm?

Yeah, sounded about right.

"Why are you here?" Aunt demanded.

"I need some information about how to reach the Unseelie Fae realm. I know that you were born there."

The spider spat on the ground—or tried to. It was clearly a human instinct that she hadn't gotten rid of yet.

Fates, this was delightful.

"Why did you leave?" I asked. "Was it because you were weak?"

I wouldn't kill her today—as long as the Unseelie magic was out of control within me, I didn't want to do anything that could be construed as evil—but that didn't mean I couldn't stab her with my words.

"I wasn't going to stick around there," she said. Fangs clicked in her mouth, and it was an eerie experience to watch her speak.

"Because of my mother?"

"Bitch." The spider tried to spit again, then looked at Tarron. "Who's this?"

He stepped forward. "Tarron, King of the Seelie Fae. And if you don't tell her what she wants to know, I'll tear you limb from limb."

The rage in his voice made me feel a bit warm, in a weirdly good way. It was almost as if he hated her, given what she'd done to me. He'd seen the dungeon after all.

"I'm not telling her anything." My aunt's keen eyes assessed me. "Perhaps a competition though."

I raised a brow.

"A race to the top of the trees. If you win, I give you what you want to know. If I win, you use your magic to turn me back and stay with me forever."

I shivered at the mere thought, then stiffened my spine. No way in hell I'd stay here with her, no matter the outcome of the race.

I was powerful. I wasn't in chains.

I'd kill her before that happened.

I caught Tarron's eye, and read the same thing on his face. He wouldn't leave me here. I could almost feel the determination in him. There was a connection between us —unlike anything I'd ever felt. I could almost read his intentions on the air. Like some sort of weird pheromone.

Had to be the fated mates bond.

"A race, you say?" I crossed my arms. "No offensive magic, just race to the tops of the trees?"

"Exactly."

The trees were tall—hundreds of feet in the air—and she was probably a good climber. A great climber. She wouldn't have chosen this if she hadn't thought she'd win.

But she didn't know how fast I was. My Dragon Blood gave me insane speed and strength—which she'd never realized because she'd kept me locked up in a cage my whole life.

"Okay." I shrugged. "Works for me."

I wasn't planning to play fair, anyway. I'd try to beat her on her terms, but if it didn't work, I had a backup.

Aunt clicked her fangs, an almost happy gesture, and I

turned to leave the cabin. The back of my neck prickled, and I looked back at her. She followed us out of the horrible little building, and I kept my gaze on her every second.

She'd always been tricky and smart. No way I'd let her get the drop on me today.

In the clearing outside the house, Aunt stopped. The trees loomed high overhead, and she pointed to two of them with one of her front legs. "Those two."

They were massive, with bark so thick and knobby I could use it for handholds. Many of the branches were wider around than the trunk of a normal tree.

"Go!" Aunt shouted, then raced forward.

She'd given me no warning this competition was even about to start, the bitch.

She was probably bored out of her mind here and just wanted to win something.

Over her dead body.

I sprinted forward, leaving Tarron on the ground. He was my backup, and I was glad to have him. I pushed myself hard, giving it every bit of speed my Dragon Blood could muster. I gained quickly on Aunt, reaching the thick trunks at the same time she did.

Aunt climbed onto the right one, so I took the left. With a leap, I jumped onto the tree and grabbed the thick bark, climbing as fast as I could.

We stayed neck and neck for the first hundred feet. Aunt had eight legs, but I had magical speed.

Sweat dampened my skin as I went higher, finally

taking the lead. Out of the corner of my vision, I could see her hiss. Her rage almost vibrated on the air.

Faster, I climbed.

I barely saw the silvery jet of spiderweb that she shot at me. I darted left, narrowly avoiding it. The sticky stuff clung to the tree.

She shot another bolt, and I darted right.

"Cheating!" I shouted. "No offensive magic."

She shot another bolt of web.

Anger surged inside me. This probably hadn't ever been a race at all. She'd just wanted to get me up here and trap me with her web. With me out of the picture, she'd take out Tarron.

Then I'd be her prisoner.

Oh, hell no.

I kept climbing—mostly to get away from her at this point—and sliced my fingertip with my sharp thumbnail. Pain flared and blood welled.

I imagined lightning, crackling and fierce. The magic filled me, welling to life so fast that it burst out of me, nearly uncontrolled. It shot toward Aunt, blasting into the tree above her.

The explosion was so bright it nearly blinded me. Thunder boomed, followed by the crack of wood breaking. When the light cleared and I could see again, I saw the top of Aunt's tree topple right, then plunge to the ground below.

Holy fates.

I hadn't meant for that to happen. The lightning bolt

had been ten times as big as I'd intended. I could have killed Aunt. Along with my only chance at getting the info I needed.

Fates, my magic was out of control. The Unseelie power within me was screwing everything up.

Aunt leapt from her tree trunk to the next one, clinging tightly as she shot another jet of web at me. It nearly hit me, brushing stickily off my hand. I yanked my hand free.

Out of the corner of my eye, on the opposite side away from Aunt, I caught sight of movement.

Spiders.

A dozen of them, each the size of a basketball. They scuttled toward me through the trees, eyes bright and fangs flashing.

Backup.

Aunt had called backup, and she was trying to surround me.

Rage and fear burst inside me, followed by magic. It swelled within me, the Unseelie side rising to the surface, fueled by my emotions.

It pulsed around my back, and my wings burst free. Sparkling and bright, they lit up the night around me. Power flowed through me, and I launched myself off the tree.

I flew toward Aunt, hurtling through the air. The Unseelie magic flickered inside me, bright then dim. My wings faltered. I slammed into Aunt and hung on, dragging her down from the tree. I tried to move my wings, but they resisted, flickering in and out of existence.

We hurtled to the ground, wind tearing at us, and I managed to shift so she was below me. We slammed onto the leaf-strewn earth, grunting.

I tried my faulty magic one last time, flicking my thumbnail over my fingertip to make it bleed. I called upon my persuasive magic, swiping my black blood across her hairy face, right between the eyes.

"Speak the truth to me," I commanded.

She hissed. "You use your magic against me?"

I grinned ferociously. "And I'm loving every second."

I was doing what I'd always wanted to do as a child, and *it felt good.*

She thrashed beneath me.

"Still," I commanded.

She stilled, mostly.

"Tarron!"

He was at my side a moment later, a rope in hand, as if he'd read my mind. I scrambled off. Quickly, he bound my aunt's legs to her body.

"How'd you get the rope?" I asked.

"I have a bit of conjuring."

"Nice." I inspected my aunt, who thrashed on the ground and glared at me, then dug into my pocket and pulled out the truth serum. I spoke softly to Tarron. "With my magic going a bit haywire, I didn't want to rely on it."

"You *didn't* mean to blow up the tree?"

"Not precisely." I walked toward Aunt, bracing myself for the job ahead. I didn't want to get near her snappy fangs, that was for sure.

I uncorked the vial and commanded, "Be still."

She fought my persuasive power, but finally stilled enough that I could pour the serum into her mouth. I yanked the vial back and stepped away.

"I'll never tell you anything," she spat.

"Yes, you will. And I should have done this right away. Now, tell me where the entrance to the Unseelie Court is."

She spat ineffectively—a nasty habit she was really going to have to get over—but finally spoke, the words forced out of her by the potion. "The entrance is at the Circle of Night, a sacred Unseelie place."

"Where is that?"

"In the Highlands."

"I'm going to need more than that to go on. The Highlands are pretty big."

"It's in the central Highlands, but that's all I know."

I frowned. It looked like the words were forced out of her. My magic might be acting weird, but the potion was infallible. She had to be telling the truth.

I looked at Tarron. "What do you think?"

"She seems like she's telling the truth, and it's more information than we had before."

"It's what Cass needed to pinpoint the location."

"It'll have to be good enough," he said.

"Help me," Aunt said. "Turn me back."

I stared at her. "No. And frankly, I'm enjoying your misery. You brought this on yourself."

"Bitch."

I grinned. "Sure, I'm cool with that."

I turned on my heel and left, leaving my aunt tied up in the forest.

Tarron joined me, and we strode from the forest.

"You're ruthless," he said.

"Can you blame me?"

"No. And I like it."

I smiled. I'd enjoyed the sight of Aunt, tied up. A spider. Miserable and alone. A perfect punishment for what she'd done. I probably should have taken a photo for Aeri.

A shriek sounded from behind us, pure rage. Pure evil.

"She's pissed." I grinned.

A rustling sound came from the forest around us. Magic filled the air with ominous intent.

"Something is coming," Tarron said.

I got the overwhelming feeling that I should start running.

Burn appeared at my side, the big thorn wolf growling low in his throat.

That was a *definite* sign that something dangerous was about to happen. Burn always showed up to have my back. It was like our souls were connected and he could sense when I was in trouble.

"Go," I said. "Run."

I'd just picked up the pace when I spotted the spiders dropping down from the trees. The same basketball-sized ones that she'd sent to hunt me earlier.

Her minions.

I drew a dagger from the ether and hurled it at one

who hung right in front of me, dangling from a long line of spiderweb. It pierced him through the belly, and he hissed, skittering back up his line.

Next to me, Burn shot thorns at the spiders scuttling along the ground. Tarron fired blasts of sunlight, making the whole forest glow. Spiders fell, but more appeared.

So many.

And they headed right for me. As if Aunt had given them special instructions.

The bitch probably had.

I threw another dagger, sprinting as fast as I could. The blade pierced the spider through the head, and it tumbled backward.

"We have to get to the exit tunnel!" I gasped. It was the only place we could transport from.

Despite Burn's best efforts, the spiders got closer, scrambling along the ground. Tarron hit the ones that descended from the trees, but he couldn't keep up. There were just so many. My lungs burned as I ran. Tarron couldn't even fly out of here because there were so many spiders hanging in the air, their nets filling the trees above.

Fates, please let us be close to the exit.

I hurled another blade, taking out a third spider, but I was running out of weapons. Dare I try to make sunlight magic the way that Tarron did? It was sending them flying.

No, too risky.

I could burn *us* to death with it if my magic went haywire.

Panting, I sprinted for the edge of the forest. I could just see it, a spot where the trees began to thin.

"Almost there," Tarron said.

Pain flared in my left calf, and I stumbled. I looked down, horrified to a see a spider with its fangs sunk deep into my leg. I drew my sword from the ether, but Burn was faster. His white jaws clamped around the spider's body and tore him off.

But it was too late.

Agony shot up my leg.

I gasped. "Poison."

I could feel it.

The horrible liquid raced through my veins, freezing up my muscles. I limped, going slower and slower. Burn growled and shot thorns at any spider that dared approach, but I was losing the ability to move.

Panic fluttered in my chest, making it hard to breathe.

We were nearly to the edge of the forest, but I couldn't run anymore. I stumbled, nearly stopping.

Tarron whirled around and raced back toward me, sweeping me up into his arms, then sprinting forward.

I clung to him. "Thank you."

He didn't respond, just ran as fast as he could, racing through the forest with the thorn wolf at his side. We reached the edge of the trees and spilled out into the tunnel that led to the main market in Grimrealm.

Heart pounding, I looked back over Tarron's shoulder.

The spiders stopped at the edge of the trees, unwilling to venture out into the main tunnel.

But then a few did, driven by Aunt's enraged screams, which I could still hear.

"They're still coming." The words were slow as they left my lips. My tongue felt numb.

The poison.

It was spreading.

Spiders advancing from behind was the last thing I saw before I passed out in Tarron's arms.

7

AGONY TORE THROUGH ME AS I OPENED MY EYES. THE ceiling soared high overhead, beautiful pale wood forming arches to support it. A fresh breeze blew across my face, smelling of night-blooming flowers.

Through bleary vision, I could see Tarron, leaning over me. Concern creased his face, and his warm hand pressed against my stomach.

"What's going on?" The words were raspy and quiet as they escaped my lips.

"Healing you." Tarron bit out the words, his attention clearly focused on the task at hand.

I closed my eyes, memories flooding through me. We had the name of the entrance to the Unseelie Court. I'd left Aunt in the forest. A spider had bitten me.

The poison.

My eyes flared open, worry tightening my chest. "Burn. Is he okay?"

"Didn't get bit. Disappeared."

The thorn wolf tended to do that. Worry alleviated, I couldn't help but focus on the pain in my leg. It was worse there, but it spread through my whole body, all the way to my head and fingers.

But Tarron's hand was a warm comfort on my stomach, his healing light flowing into me. It drove away the pain, fighting it back inch by inch. He was neutralizing the poison, somehow.

As the pain faded, pleasure took its place. The absence of pain could feel like pleasure, true. But this was more than that.

It was being close to Tarron. Feeling his touch on my skin. His hand on my body.

I drew in a slow breath, relieved to find that the horrible stench the potion had given us had gone away. All I could smell was the fresh forest scent of Tarron's magic and the distinctly masculine scent of his skin.

He was so close that I could see the light gleaming on his hair and the amazing green of his eyes. Full lips and sharp cheekbones.

He really was perfect.

His broad shoulders blocked out the light, and as desire replaced the pain, I longed to reach up and touch him. It was the strangest thing, how his healing touch made me feel like I knew him. It created a connection between us—one that I liked.

We might not trust each other. We might be fighting the connection between us.

But our bodies weren't.

"How are you feeling?" His voice was strained from the effort, and he didn't let up on his work.

"A lot better. Pain's almost gone." It was only in my leg, now.

It had faded enough that I could ignore it.

My gaze riveted to his lips as thoughts swirled in my mind.

I didn't even know if he liked me, but I couldn't help it.

He'd destroyed the dungeon that had kept me caged as a child. He had saved me from the spiders.

When the last of the pain faded and my skin had knit back together, he removed his hand. I nearly gasped at the loss of the warmth. But he hovered over me, his body curled almost protectively over top of mine.

His gaze met mine, and I wasn't shocked to see heat there. Desire. His eyes were already shifting from black to green.

I couldn't feel this so strongly for someone who felt nothing in return.

My palms itched to reach for him. To clutch him close and run my hands over the hard muscles of his shoulders and arms.

"Mari." His voice was low, rough. His gaze traveled over my face, down to my chest, then back up to my eyes. "Remove the glamour."

I blinked.

"You still have red hair."

Ah. I let the magic fade from me, retuning me to

normal. It hardly seemed possible, but he looked even more torn up. Like he wanted to ravish me.

"You prefer me with black hair?" I asked, remembering how his eyes had once darkened with desire at the sight of me in my plunging dress and with my makeup and hair done to the extreme. "And made up?"

"I like you however you want to be." Truth vibrated in the words. I liked myself in my extreme disguise, so he liked it too.

His scent wrapped around me. He was so close that I could feel the heat of his skin.

Every inch of me vibrated with tension. With suppressed longing.

I moved for him at the same time he moved for me. We collided in a rush of desire, his lips crushing mine. I parted my lips, moaning, and he devoured my mouth.

His skilled lips moved over mine. He nipped, then licked. Brushed, then drove deep.

My head spun and my body heated.

With shaking hands, I reached for his waist, my finger-tips finding bare, hot skin. I ran my hands over the hard muscles to his back, unable to get enough of him. He arched into my touch, as if he never wanted me to stop.

With a groan, he moved his lips to the side of my neck. He trailed kisses down the sensitive skin, occasionally scraping with his teeth.

Had his fangs appeared?

I shivered at the thought.

He bit down lightly, not breaking the skin but hard

enough to make desire flash hotly through me. I pressed closer toward him. His hand dipped beneath the hemline of my shirt and brushed against my waist. It moved toward my chest, and I ached for his touch.

More.

Heat rushed through me as I pulled him down on top of me, my head spinning at the heavy press of his body against mine.

He groaned. "Mari."

He'd shifted fully, his eyes black and his horns silver. White canines had sharpened into fangs, and he was so sexy I felt like I was burning alive. His desire for me lit me up inside.

I spread my legs, welcoming him close.

Tarron held himself over me, pressing against my most sensitive places. Pleasure shot through my veins like fire. He moved against me in the most incredible rhythm, making desire coil tight inside me.

I arched, trying to give him space to touch more of my bare skin.

There was too much clothing between us. I wanted to take it off, but I was too busy running my hands over his strong arms and back, trying to touch as much of him as I could. He caged me in with his hands, his lips trailing down my neck and pressing hot kisses to the sensitive skin.

Everything tightened inside me, desire threatening to make me explode. I'd just wrapped my legs around his hips when a loud knock sounded at the door.

He cursed and pulled his mouth away from my chest.

"Tell them to go away," I said.

The knock sounded again.

He groaned, sounding torn.

Knock.

"Can't." Slowly, he drew himself away from me.

Cool air rushed over my skin, making my head clear again. I sat up and shook my head. Fates, he was right. Of course he couldn't tell them to go away. We were on a deadline, trying to stop a tragedy.

My heart rate still thundered as I watched him walk to the door.

How the hell had I let that happen? I had no control where he was concerned. All I knew for certain about him was that he didn't hate me and he believed I didn't actively try to sabotage his kingdom.

That wasn't a great reason to fall into bed with someone.

It had to be the Fated Mate bond. It was a problem.

Except...

I wanted him more than I'd ever wanted anyone. The chemistry was off the charts.

That was a pretty good reason to fall into bed with someone.

I straightened my hair and stood, relieved to find that there was no pain at all in my leg. As subtly as I could, I moved toward the mirror to make sure I didn't look like I felt—hot as hell and ready to get down.

My bare face stared back at me, and I twitched in surprise.

I'd forgotten that I wasn't wearing my usual mask of black paint. And my hair was flat. No bouffant, no lift. Nothing.

Ugh.

I waved a hand over my face, and the black sweep of makeup appeared around my eyes. My hair got a little lift, too, and I suddenly looked like the badass I usually was.

Better.

I turned back to the door to see Tarron welcome Cass into the room. He'd gotten rid of any trace of his fae shift.

"Cass! How did you get here?"

She pointed to Tarron. "He called me while you were unconscious. Del dropped me off. She's waiting for me at a pub back in Scotland."

Her sister Del had transport magic like me. "Thank you for coming."

"Tarron said you might have the information I needed to locate the entrance to the Unseelie Court."

"I hope so. My aunt said that the entrance is within the Circle of Night," I said. "It's supposed to be in the central Highlands."

She nodded. "Okay, that might help." She reached out her hand. "Give me your hand anyway. You're technically from there, so it might help as well."

I gripped her hand and waited, my breath held. If this worked, I'd take great satisfaction in knowing that Aunt had given me the name that had helped me find the place where I could fix my magic. She'd hate knowing that.

Her magic surged on the air as she worked. Finally, her

eyes popped open. "It's located at the peak of Mount Schiehallion."

"That's a mouthful."

"It sure is." A musical voice sounded from behind Cass.

I dropped her hands and looked over her shoulder to see Arrowen, the old Fae seer, walk into the room. She was beautiful in an ageless way, her pale white hair shining in the light. Her silver dress made her sparkle as she glided into the room.

Her gaze fell on me. "I thought you'd be back."

"I am. My friend here was just helping us."

Cass turned to meet her.

"Oh, I know your friend." Arrowen's eyes gleamed with knowledge. "Very powerful, that one. Messy past, though."

"You're telling me," Cass said. She turned to me. "If you don't need any more help, I'll get out of here and have a drink with Del."

"Thanks, Cass. You're a lifesaver."

"It's amazing how even a little clue can jumpstart my gift. I know it wasn't easy to go back there. Good job finding it. And good luck."

"Thanks."

She left, and I turned to Tarron and Arrowen.

"I invited her to see if she could scry for any information about the Circle of Night."

"He says that's the name of the entrance to the Unseelie Court," Arrowen said. "I've looked for them before with no luck. Perhaps this information will give my gift enough help that I can see a bit more. Names are powerful, you see."

"Anything you can tell us would be helpful," I said.

"Give me a moment." She drifted to Tarron's huge chair. It sat in front of the window, a massive throne that overlooked his domain.

He said nothing as she sat on the chair, but then, he really didn't seem like the sort to be bothered by an old woman sitting on his throne. He wore his power on his person, not in symbols.

Arrowen's magic filled the air, delicate and bright. She closed her eyes, and her skin glowed with radiance.

The thought drifted away as I watched her work, tension filling the air. A few minutes later, her blue eyes popped open.

"Well?" Tarron asked.

"Great danger resides there."

Of course that would be the first thing she'd say. It was just how my luck was running lately. Also, it was pretty obvious. Not that I was going to say it.

"It's located at the top of one of the highest peaks."

"Mount Schiehallion," Tarron said.

"Yes, the peak closest to the moon and the lightning."

That was a very Fae thing to say, but we needed more precise directions. "What else can you tell us about it?"

"You must approach the circle at dawn or dusk, as the day fades or rises," Arrowen said.

Yeah, that sounded about right for the Fae.

"However, it will always be slightly dark there," she

continued. "Fraught with dangerous magic that you cannot navigate on your own. You will need help."

"From who?" Tarron asked.

"I saw four stags in my vision. The noble stags of the Four Rivers. They are the only ones who can navigate the dangerous terrain. They live at the base of the mountain and will come to your aid if you bring them rowan berries."

"We'll bring them a wagon full," Tarron said.

The seer nodded. "Ride the stags to the circle. Once you've arrived, you'll have to find a way to enter." Her face turned serious. "Unfortunately, that is the bit I cannot see."

"We'll figure it out," I said. "What do we do once we're there?"

"You must find the Evil Eye."

"Is that a person or a thing?" I asked.

"An Unseelie Fae with a seer's gift."

"She sounds like a peach," I said.

"Is there anything else?" Tarron asked.

"You'll want to appear as an Unseelie Fae when you enter their realm. Fortunately, you're both dark-haired and pale-skinned. A bit of potion should help you blend better. I will send Luna up with it in a few hours."

"No sooner?" Tarron asked.

"It will take some time to brew. But trust me, you will want it. Blending with their kind will make your task far easier."

"Thank you, Arrowen." Tarron nodded.

She rose and moved to depart. After she'd left, Tarron

turned to me. "You should practice your wings. If you can use them in the Unseelie realm, you'll have an advantage."

I frowned. I *wanted* to practice. I'd nearly gotten them to work back at Aunt's horrible little hovel. But I didn't know how.

"They only come out when I'm in danger or need help."

"That won't do. You need to be able to control their appearance. Going to the Unseelie Court will help you get your magic under control, but you may need your wings before then."

"And they'd help me blend in among their kind." Not to mention, I needed to learn sooner rather than later how to control my gifts.

"Let me help you." Tarron approached to stand in front of me.

"How?"

"I'll need to touch you." He raised his hands and hovered them over my shoulders.

Memories of our kiss flashed in my mind, and his scent wrapped around me. My breath grew short.

"Okay." The word barely escaped my lips.

He rested his strong hands on my shoulders, and heat shot through me. I looked up, meeting his green gaze. Desire flashed in his eyes, then disappeared as if he were wrestling it under control.

He frowned. "Are you afraid?"

"No."

"You sure? Feels a bit like you're afraid of this new magic."

"I'm afraid of my lack of control." I scoffed. "You've seen what I did. Wouldn't you be scared?"

"You've used your other magic since then and been fine."

"Mostly. I've stuck to magic I'm pretty familiar with, so that helps. But this new stuff is scary."

He nodded as if he got it. "You'll get better. But you need to stop being afraid."

"Just tell me what to do. I want to try."

"Feel my magic. I'm going to call upon my wings. Feel what my magic does, and try to replicate it."

Magic was a resource that existed inside all supernaturals. We had it in different quantities and styles, but we all used it in basically the same ways. We called it up from inside our souls, from deep within our bodies. Then we manipulated it and used it, creating the skills and powers that each of us was known for.

By touching Tarron, I could more easily feel the magic inside him. It was powerful, bucking like a wild stallion. He had amazing control of it as he called it to his uses. I could almost feel my back tingle as he directed his magic toward his wings. They flared back behind him, like silver lightning. Magnificent.

I gasped. "I can feel it."

He nodded. "You try."

It was so strange how touching him made it easier for me to mimic what he did with his magic. I tried it with my own, calling upon the power that shimmered restlessly inside me. At first, it resisted. The Fae power that was so new was used to doing what it wanted. But *I* needed to control it.

I imagined my silvery, ephemeral wings growing from my back. I pictured the magic flowing through my soul and going to my shoulder blades, creating my new gift and letting it flare to life behind me.

As if following my command, it burst from me. My wings sparkled, magic and power glowing bright.

My gaze flashed up to Tarron's. "It worked."

Pride gleamed in his gaze, along with more heat than I'd ever seen. "You're magnificent."

Warmth filled me. No one had ever called me magnificent before. I agreed, truth be told. But I liked hearing it from him.

My gaze dropped to his lips, and heat surged between us. I could see in his eyes that he was thinking the same thing I was.

Then he shook his head, fighting it. "Now send them away."

I cleared my throat, forcing my mind away from kisses. We didn't have time for that. No matter how drawn to each other we were—there was clearly *no* fighting this fated mate bond—we were trying to save Magic's Bend.

From *my* fuck-up.

I drew in a steadying breath and tried to force the magic down inside me. Tried to retract my wings. I'd need full control in the Unseelie Court. If not of all my magic, then at least of my wings.

Lack of control was my nemesis these days, and I'd fight it.

After a bit of effort, my wings retracted back inside my body.

"Good." Tarron withdrew his hands, and I nearly swayed toward him to keep his touch on me.

I mentally cursed myself for my extreme lack of chill.

"Now try it without my touch."

I nodded, and gave it my best effort.

No doubt about it, this was a hell of a lot harder. Without having his magic to mirror, it was far more difficult. My wings flickered at my back, coming out only a bit.

Frustration spiked within me. If I couldn't do a little thing like call upon my wings, there was no way I could get a handle on the rest of the Unseelie magic that was inside me. "I need to visit the Unseelie realm. I can *feel* how broken the magic is inside me."

Tarron frowned and nodded. "But you're getting better. Try again."

I did. It took too long, but this time, the wings came out in full.

"Good," he said. "In an emergency, your wings will probably come to you faster."

I sure hoped so.

"You need to rest," he said. "We don't have long, but you need to recoup some of your magic after what we just went through. We have a few hours before we need to set out for the stone circle if we're going to make it at dusk when it opens."

I didn't know how I could possibly rest, but he had a point. I'd used quite a lot of power in Grimrealm, and I was totally beat.

"You can have my bed," he said.

I was about to point out that it was a big bed—we could both surely sleep in it—but kept my mouth shut. If we were both on that bed, we wouldn't be sleeping. And the last thing I needed to be doing was having sex instead of saving Magic's Bend.

That would be a bad look.

And also damn me to hell.

"Thanks." I strode to the bed and kicked off my boots. As I climbed beneath the covers, he went to the huge chair in front of the window and slouched low, clearly intending to fall asleep.

He waved his hand, and the fairy lights in the ceiling dimmed. I struggled to rest, listening instead for the slightest movement from Tarron.

Finally, darkness sucked me in, and I slept hard.

Until the comms charm around my neck flared to life, and Aeri's voice came out. "Mari? You need to get over here. To the chasm. Quick."

I jerked upright in bed. "Shit, what's wrong?"

"The chasm is changing. Faster." Panic sounded in her voice.

"Be there soon." My gaze flashed to Tarron, who had surged to his feet. "How long till you're ready?"

"Let me check on that serum that Arrowen was making."

As if she'd heard him speak, there was a knock at the door. He strode over and swung it open.

Luna stood on the other side, her blue hair pulled into a high ponytail. Her pink eyes flashed between me in the bed and Tarron at the door, then she winked. "Special delivery."

"Thank you." Tarron took something from her and shut the door in her face.

"Rude!" Her voice filtered through the door, and I would have smiled if I weren't so stressed.

I climbed out of bed and grabbed a butterscotch candy from my pocket, then shoved it into my mouth. As I chomped down on the hard candy, I pushed my feet into my boots.

Tarron walked toward me and handed me a small vial, along with an obsidian dagger. "They're the signature weapon of the Unseelie Fae. It will help to have one."

"Great."

"Give me a moment." He disappeared through a small door, then returned two minutes later, dressed entirely in black like an Unseelie.

"Come this way." He led me to an alcove off the large room, where a glowing portal shimmered in the air. "This leads directly to earth."

"So we can bypass the damned guard in the forest?" I was still pissed about her knocking me unconscious. He was the one to blame, but I wasn't keen on seeing her anyhow.

"Precisely."

"Good."

"Just imagine where you want to go."

"Same place as before, a few streets over from the edge of the chasm."

He nodded and stepped in. I followed, picturing the quiet city street. The ether sucked me in and spat me out right next to Tarron. The air prickled with magic, dark and foreboding. From a few streets over, I could hear the faint hum of activity. I shivered, horrified by what I'd caused.

Then I shoved the thought aside and focused on the job at hand. "Let's go."

We strode down the street, headed toward the chaos on the west side. When we reached the end of the alley that led to the chasm, I hesitated, inspecting the scene.

There were dozens of Order of the Magica members there, all working to keep the chasm contained. They stood positioned at the edges, their robes flapping in the wind as they directed their magic toward the deep pit that stretched all the way down the street. Dark magic pulsed from it, almost familiar.

I looked down the street in either direction. As if she sensed my arrival, Aeri looked up from her position about twenty yards down the street. Her pale blond hair glinted in the light of the street lamps. She hurried toward me, tapping a tall, robed woman on the shoulder as she ran.

They appeared in front of us a moment later.

I drew in a steadying breath at the sight of Rose, one of the members of the Council of Demon Slayers. Her cloak covered her face—it always did—but her magical signature and voice were distinct. All of the council members were concealed by cloaks, but their magic spoke for itself. They had the signatures of those whose life mission was to help the world. They inspired feelings of kindness, respect, comfort, and compassion.

Normally, standing in front of her would make me feel better.

Not today.

Council members almost never left their headquarters, but here she was.

Which meant this was *bad*.

I'd already known it was bad, but this was like a big neon sign saying *Mordaca, you've fucked up totally*.

Got it, thanks.

"Rose." I inclined my head.

"Mordaca." Her voice resonated with power. And disappointment.

"I'm sorry about this." I gestured to the chasm.

"It's...not good." She turned to look at the Order members trying to keep control of the chasm. "We're keeping things under control here. We've had to pull some serious strings, but the Order of the Magica isn't asking questions. At our request. It's the only time we can pull that string, and we're using it for you."

I swallowed hard, both grateful for the fact that they were covering for me and honored. And also guilty as hell.

"But we need you to fix this," Rose said. "*Soon.* You're the only one who can."

I nodded.

"What's the problem now?" Tarron asked, clearly not here to waste time hearing me get a lecture from my boss. "Why did you call us?"

Rose gestured to the chasm. "The magical energy has changed. Become clearer. There's demonic energy there, but also something different. We want to see if Mordaca recognizes it. If there's anything she can do with her magic to stabilize it." Her gaze sharpened on Tarron. "And you as well, King of the Seelie Fae. It's really going out of control now, and we need all the help we can get."

I nodded and stepped up to the chasm, peering into the depths.

The dark magic seeped from deep within the chasm, a black mist that reeked of a familiar scent—brimstone and putrid night lilies.

I gaped and stumbled back. "It's Unseelie power."

It was my *mother's*.

8

THE DARK MAGIC SEEPING FROM THE CHASM WASN'T ONLY demonic.

It was also Unseelie.

For some reason, it was easier to read now. As the chasm grew wider and the magic seeped out ever faster, it became more obvious.

And somehow, my mother was involved. Her magical signature was here, along with a demonic signature. Had she sent the strange demon that I'd fought with?

There was a puzzle here, but I couldn't quite put the pieces together.

My gaze flashed to Aeri's, and she nodded, her expression serious. She recognized the scent as well. Somehow, my mother had something to do with this.

But what?

"This is the same dark magic that polluted my realm."

Tarron frowned. "With the addition of demon magic. Underworld magic."

"It's a totally different scenario, but there's a connection," I said. No way I'd mention my mother now. I needed his help to fix this, and I couldn't drive him off if he hated me for what my mother had done. Or worse, thought I played some role in it because we were related. Guilt tugged at me, and I looked away from him. "There has to be."

"Our mages are keeping the magic repressed and slowing its spread, but their resources aren't limitless," Rose said. "Is there anything you can do to freeze it while you hunt for the solution? At least temporarily?"

"We can try," I said. Though I had no freaking clue how I'd do it. I looked at Tarron. "Can you stop the earth from splitting?"

"For a little while, perhaps. I didn't try it earlier because it's a temporary measure, but maybe every little bit helps."

"It has to," Aeri said. "Just try. And then you will go to the Unseelie Court?"

"We've found it." I was more determined than ever to go and master my magic so I could scrub this Unseelie stink from the earth and Tarron could knit it back together for good.

Tarron held out his hand, and I gripped it.

A shiver ran up my arm as I drew in a steady breath and did what I always did when I tried new magic.

I winged it.

So much of magic was uncharted territory. We knew a lot about it, but it was ever evolving and changing. I did my best to connect with the dark magic in the chasm. It made my stomach heave and my skin chill, but I had to understand it to modify it.

Finally, I made a connection with it.

Next to me, I could feel Tarron's earth magic pouring out of him, into the ground. He was slowly dragging the torn earth back together, but the dark magic was fighting him. I had to remove it before he could do what he really needed to do.

Except I couldn't. The best I could do was force the dark magic a little deeper into the earth. Together, we managed to partially stabilize the chasm and buy the mages a bit more time.

Panting, I stepped back and dropped Tarron's hand. "That should help a bit."

Rose leaned over and peered down into the chasm. "You do have a knack for that kind of thing."

Dark magic, she meant.

But I wouldn't take it personally. I was born with it, and it was a bit, ah...*weird.* But I wouldn't use it for evil, so it would all be okay. The Council of Demon Slayers wouldn't kick me out. And the Order of the Magica wouldn't figure out what I was...or what I'd done here.

And I'd just tell myself that until I believed it. Easypeasy.

I turned to Rose. "We need to go now. But we'll be back as soon as we can."

"Hurry." The direness of the situation was clear in her voice, and I nodded.

Tarron looked at me. "I have a transport charm. We'll use it to get to the edge of Mount Schiehallion so that you can save your magic."

I nodded, grateful. I had a hell of a lot of the stuff, but I'd need to conserve it if we were pulling a rogue operation in Unseelie territory.

Aeri hugged me tight, whispering, "Be careful with him. The way he looks at you makes me nervous."

"How so?"

"Like he's going to eat you alive."

"He might, actually." I pulled back and stepped away, then joined Tarron.

His energy prickled against my skin as I stood close. He threw the small transport charm to the ground. As soon as the little rock hit the pavement, a silvery cloud of smoke burst upward.

Tarron reached for my hand, then gripped my smaller one in his far larger. A shiver raced up my arm, and together, we stepped through the portal. As the ether sucked me in and spun me through space, I let Tarron choose our final location.

We appeared at the base of a mountain that was shrouded in mist. The sage green slopes were speckled with rocks, and the darkened sky made it hard to see. At our backs, a forest loomed.

We were about an hour from sunset, which didn't give us much time to reach the Circle of Night.

"Give me a moment." Tarron stepped aside, and his magic flared to life. A moment later, a huge cart full of rowan berries appeared in front of him. They glistened in the faint light that filtered through the heavy clouds.

"Noble stags!" Tarron's voice boomed toward the forest. "We seek your aid and bring an offering."

I waited, my skin tight and muscles tense. *Please show.*

I scanned the forest, and finally, a bush rustled to my right. An enormous stag stepped through. It was far larger than any I'd ever seen, the size of a huge stallion. Massive horns extended up from its head, and its brilliant russet coat gleamed under the light.

Though it was still forty yards away, I could feel its magic even from here. A sense of noble power and a peaceful spirit. It calmed me, settling my nerves for the first time in what felt like a century.

A moment later, another appeared. It had a paler coat, though it was just as big and magnificent.

"They're interested," Tarron murmured. "They just need to approve of us."

"What can we do to convince them?"

He shrugged. "Nothing, really."

Tension tightened the air. Then the stags approached, their strides graceful and confident. These were not beasts to run from a confrontation.

They walked up to the cart full of berries and sniffed it delicately, then turned to Tarron and me.

"We need to get to the stone circle at the top of the mountain," I said. "And we request your help."

The darker stag bobbed its head in understanding. Together, the two noble beasts approached us and bent on their front legs.

The palest one was near me, so I climbed onto the back and rubbed the graceful neck. "Thank you."

The stag snuffled out a breath, then began to walk. Tarron caught up to me quickly, not so much guiding his mount as riding along gracefully. He looked as noble and powerful as the king he was.

"You're a natural," I said.

"All the Fae are."

"And the king, even more so."

He inclined his head, but it was clear the title didn't sit easily on his shoulders. "Sorry. I know you don't want to be."

"It's not so much that. It's a responsibility that I carry with honor." He hesitated a moment, and I knew what he'd say next. "It's that I'd rather my brother be here instead."

"I know."

"I need to come to terms with it." The agony in his voice surprised me. He'd never shown me so much emotion. Besides when he wanted to kiss me, of course. And that was another kind of emotion altogether.

"I used the best of everything in my attempts to save him," he said. "But we weren't strong enough, and the curse took him instead. I know I need to accept that."

"I think it'll grow easier with time." I wondered if the

Fae had therapy. I had a hard time imagining him spilling his guts to a stranger, but it could be good for him.

He nodded, giving me a small smile. "So will your magic."

"I hope so." The stag sidestepped an invisible obstacle, and I tightened my legs to stay on. "I just want to finish this damned thing and get back to normal."

Tarron's stag shied to the right, and mine followed. The magic in the air changed, growing more threatening as we ascended. It prickled sharply against my skin.

"We're getting to the iffy bit," I said.

The stags began to walk in a zigzag pattern, avoiding threats that we couldn't see. There were boulders scattered here and there, along with a few lone, twisted trees. But otherwise, the hillside was barren.

A chill blasted from my right, and the stag veered away. Farther up, a sense of foreboding came from the left, and the animal avoided it cleanly. The higher we got, the more the stag darted and dodged.

The mist grew thicker and colder, bringing with it more threatening magic. I could hear the sound of rocks smashing together, but couldn't see them. The stag beneath me leapt high into the air, and I clung to the stag's neck, holding on tightly.

Not being able to see the threats made my heart pound so hard I thought it might pop out of my chest.

Tarron rode his steed at my side, keeping close. When the creatures began to run, I held on tightly. Wind tore at my hair as our mounts veered and weaved, and I nearly fell off twice.

In front of us, thorns grew up from the ground. Thick and twisted, they created a wall. It rose ten feet in the air. Fifteen.

The stags hesitated.

This was a threat I could see.

That was different.

The stags clearly didn't like it.

Heartbeat thundering, I shouted to Tarron, "I don't think they can jump it!"

"They can't." He raised his hands, his magic flaring, then directed his power toward the wall of thorns.

They withered into the ground, and the stags surged forward, leaping over the rubble of dead, twisted vines. My mount landed hard on the other side, and the breath whooshed out of me. I clung tightly, barely managing to hold on, and the crazy ride continued.

Finally, we reached the top of the mountain. The wind whipped across the peak, driving gusts of clouds in front of us. It was nearly impossible to see where the sun was setting as there was nothing but a pale, diffused glow.

Eerie, really.

Tarron leapt off his stag gracefully, looking perfectly windblown and handsome. He was a natural.

I grumbled as I dismounted mine, nearly falling. I stiffened my spine, mortified.

That was *so* not like me.

I was grace personified.

Normally.

But right now, my legs were killing me from the wild ride up the mountainside. If I was a Fae, I wasn't a very good one, because riding stags was freaking hard.

I turned to the beautiful beast that'd carried me safely up the mountain. "Thank you."

The graceful animal inclined its head, then turned and raced down the mountain. Tarron's stag followed, and we turned toward the stone circle.

Magic pulsed from the stones that speared the evening sky. They were jagged and sharp, and several looked to be weeping a dark oil that glimmered in the diffused light.

So, this was my heritage.

Fabulous.

"Now or never," I muttered.

I approached quickly, determined to get it over with. At the boundary of the stone circle, I stopped and carefully stuck my hand out. If I was going to be zapped by protective magic, I didn't want to get blasted in the face. Next to me, Tarron did the same.

The magic that flowed between the stones stung, but didn't hurt abominably. Carefully, I stepped through, shivering at the cold that raced over my skin.

In the middle of the circle, an enormous flat stone lay against the ground. It was carved with the most incredible, intricate Celtic knot I'd ever seen. There were hundreds, maybe thousands, of thin lines twisting and turning across the surface that was as big as my living room.

Awed, I stepped up to it. "Holy fates, I've never seen anything like this."

"It's a gate of some kind. A lock." Tarron knelt and ran a hand over one of the intricate stone lines. "We Fae love our puzzles."

"How do we open it?"

"No idea. It's the kind of thing that an Unseelie Fae would be taught from birth, so that they could come and go from their homeland. Like our gate."

I nodded, thinking about how instinct had driven me to open the gate to the Seelie Court. Maybe that same instinct could work here, too. I was Unseelie, after all.

I strode around the stone, inspecting it from all angles. The thin carved rock twisted and turned, a maze with no beginning or end.

Except...

What if that was the puzzle? I had to find the beginning and the end. Perhaps they were one and the same, and it was impossible to see it.

"I've got an idea." It took me a good twenty minutes— every one of which was stressful because we had a strict deadline—but finally, I found it.

The beginning of the knot was also the end, and the spot was marked only by a faint pulse of energy. I could feel it when I ran my hand over the stone. "Do you feel it?"

Tarron hovered his hand in the same place. "I don't."

I could because I was Unseelie.

"It's almost sunset, isn't it?" I could sense it.

"It is. In one minute, the sun will touch the horizon."

"You can feel it that clearly?"

He shrugged. "Fae gift."

It was time, then.

Instinct drove my next actions. I raised my hand and sliced my fingertip with my sharp thumbnail. A drop of midnight blood splashed to the stone, absorbing quickly into the rock.

"Unseelie blood." His eyes flashed to mine. "I didn't realize you had their blood."

My heart rate spiked. "I didn't know what it meant."

"Really?"

"Really. I mean, I knew it came from my mother and my aunt said it made me evil, but..."

"She was already trying to manipulate you and kept you in a dungeon. How were you to know if it was true?" He nodded understandingly.

He believed me.

I didn't want to be happy about it. Not when I knew that there was still a huge lie hanging between us. But I was.

I cut my finger deeper, spilling a few more droplets of blood on the stone. I'd counted thirteen in total by the time the magic sparked on the air.

"Here it goes." I lunged backward as magic swirled around us.

A portal opened in front of Tarron and me, shimmering and gray.

Tarron dug into his pocket and pulled out the potion that was meant to make us blend with the Unseelie. I did the same, then swigged it back. I winced at the foul taste—fishy and sour—then shivered as the magic raced through me.

Tarron transformed before my eyes. He still looked like himself, but his dark hair became even blacker, his skin paler. His green eyes turned to midnight, and his cheekbones cut deeply. All of his features sharpened, and though he looked a bit different, he was just as beautiful.

"Do I look different?"

"Yes." His gaze flicked over me. "Like yourself, but sharper. Harder."

I nodded. "Good. Let's go."

I made sure that the obsidian blade Luna had given me was displayed in its thigh holster, then stepped through the portal.

The ether sucked me in and spun me through space, making my heart race and my head pound. It spat me out in the middle of a dark forest, not terribly dissimilar from the one at the Seelie Court. The trees were huge here as well, but their trunks were blackened with silver leaves. Dark magic hung in the air, though it wasn't as terrible as I'd expected.

Tarron appeared next to me, his stance ready.

"Who goes there?" a voice boomed from the shadows about fifteen feet away.

I spun, turning to see a guard appear from the shadows. He was as pale-skinned and dark-haired as Tarron, with sharply pointed ears that peeked out from behind his hair. His clothing was all black, with finely embroidered sleeves and neckline. The obsidian sword at his side glinted in the diffuse light that sparkled through the tree leaves.

"Just returning home," I said, trying to sound casual.

The guard strode forward, his stiff stance loosening as he got close enough to see that we looked like Unseelie Fae.

"I don't recognize you," he said.

"It's been a while since we've passed through here," Tarron said. His kingly bearing made the guard quail a bit, and I nearly grinned.

Then the guard scowled. "I recognize everyone." He leaned forward, sniffing the air. "Magic smells funny."

"I don't know—"

He reached for his sword, cutting off my words. I smacked his hand hard, sending the blade spinning.

"You bitch," he hissed, raising his hands and calling upon his magic, so fast on the draw that he caught me by surprise. He blasted a powerful electric current right at us.

He was so close that there would be no dodging him.

Panic flared in my chest. I braced for impact.

The electric current slammed right into me, strong enough to kill me. Instead, it lit me up like a live wire and shot right out of me, rebounding to the Fae who'd attacked.

The current hit him full on, making him shake and drop to the ground.

"Crap!" I fell to my knees at his side, pressing my hands

to his chest as I checked for any signs of life. "Can you help him?"

"Why? He shot to kill."

"I want to question him about where to find the seer that Arrowen told us to visit."

He nodded sharply and pressed his hands to the man's chest. The Fae gasped, his eyes fluttering open. He still looked half dead.

"I don't know how long I can hold him." Tarron grunted.

Quickly, I sliced my fingertip with my thumbnail and swiped black blood across his forehead. "Tell us where to find the Evil Eye."

The man groaned, words tearing free of his throat. "West of town, violet house. Third level."

That made no sense to me, but the man's eyes rolled back in his head a moment later.

Tarron withdrew his hands. "That was the best I could do."

I nodded, sitting back on my heels. "We have some idea of where to go, at least."

"And some idea of what your new power is."

"Yeah." Apparently I could reflect magic back at people. Somehow. The magic had ignited inside me now that I was here in the Unseelie Court.

I'd just have to get control of it.

9

Tarron used his magic to bury the body of the fallen guard in a deep pit, then we set off toward the Unseelie Court. The forest was unusually quiet, with no sound of animals or insects. Birds with midnight blue feathers fluttered between the trees, but they moved like silent ghosts.

It was an eerie quiet that crawled over my skin, raising the hairs on the backs of my arms. It took everything I had to keep my footsteps silent on the fallen leaves. We stayed just off the main path in case anyone was coming, considering that our disguises might not hold up if we were forced to make conversation.

"We might look like Unseelie, but I don't think we act like it," I murmured to Tarron.

"Agreed. We need to avoid their kind."

The forest was smaller than the one in the Seelie realm, and we reached the edge quickly. A huge town sprawled out in front of us, accessible by a path through a meadow. The town itself rose tall into the air, the darkly fanciful buildings constructed on top of each other like an extremely decorative cake. Arched bridges soared through the night sky, connecting different structures.

Bright stars sparkled in a navy blue sky overhead, and the whole place was really quite beautiful. Though dark magic rolled out from it, the effect wasn't terrible.

"How do we tell which side of town is west?" I asked, recalling what the guard had said about the location of the seer. "There's no sun to navigate by. And those stars don't look like the ones on earth."

"They'd have a way to determine that. But I've no idea what it is."

"Let's circle the town, then. There looks to be a road on the outside edge. The guard said it was on the perimeter. I don't see many—or any—lavender houses."

"Good plan."

We set off through the meadow, the tall grasses waving in the faint breeze around us. The town grew ever closer, soaring high in the sky. Was my mother really in there somewhere? Could she sense me? Did she ever think about me?

She'd been a distant threat until now, but I couldn't help but want to meet her.

Even if she was evil.

A silly part of me hoped I'd find it was all a big misunderstanding. But it would never happen.

We reached the edge of town, and some of the tension in my shoulders receded. "No guards or gatehouse."

"Like my realm. We don't really expect people to make it this far."

"They never saw me coming."

He gave me a wry smile. "No one ever does, I imagine."

I took that to be a compliment, and headed to the right, sticking to the perimeter road that bordered the town. To my left, the buildings soared high into the sky, each little structure connected by stairs and bridges. The trim work around the houses was elaborately scrolled, and the windows glowed like golden jewels. I could sense the hustle and bustle of life in the city, but we didn't see many people standing on the little balconies that jutted out from the houses.

Again, I was struck by the fact that the place wasn't totally evil. Just a bit dark.

What was the deal?

We were about a quarter of the way around the town when I spotted the little purple house halfway up. It was a pale lavender color—the only one of its kind—and magic swirled around the exterior.

I pointed. "There's our seer."

"Strange that her magic is lavender when most everything here is dark."

"It allows her to stand out, at least. Maybe it's a calling card, meant to draw people to her." Seers were usually good business people, selling their ability to tell the future or the past.

"This way." Tarron moved toward a narrow flight that curled upward through the houses. It twisted left and right, weaving around protruding buildings and arching as a bridge over a sharply steepled roof.

I followed, hurrying past doorways and windows without looking in. The last thing we needed to do was draw attention here. I'd speak to the seer because I had to, but I was prepared to use my magic to make her cooperate. If a ton of these Unseelie figured out we were intruders...

We couldn't take them all.

Finally, we reached the door of the purple house. The magic that swirled around the facade was a faint lavender smoke, and I worked hard not to draw it in.

Tentatively, I knocked on the lavishly carved door.

It swung open immediately, revealing a wall of a man. The Unseelie Fae who stood before us was easily the biggest I'd ever seen. He was even bigger than Tarron, but he didn't look half as lethal. His face was blunt and squashed, not possessing an ounce of the scary beauty of the Fae.

Still...

Those meat hammer hands could definitely crush my skull.

I stepped back. "We're here to see the seer."

"Not without an appointment," the Fae grumbled. "And you don't have one."

Damn. I wasn't in the mood to fight. I glanced at Tarron, who looked ready to take on the guard.

"Stop it, Eotorn," a creaky voice whispered from within. "I want to see this one."

"What?" Eotorn sounded confused.

"I've been expecting her!"

What?

There was more at play here than I'd realized.

"Let her in!" the old woman demanded. I couldn't see her, but it was easy to assume she was older, given the creakiness of her voice.

Eotorn grumbled but moved aside, and I stepped into the apartment, my skin chilling as I entered the seer's lair. The walls were covered entirely in living black vines. They moved like snakes, and for a moment, I thought they were.

I flinched back from one that reached out to touch my shoulder.

"They won't hurt you." The voice came from the shadows.

I turned to look, spotting the older woman sitting by the fire. She wore a lavender gown, and her skin glowed pale white. Black hair flowed down her shoulders without a hint of gray, but her face was so deeply lined that she couldn't be a day under a hundred. Delicate antlers extended from her head. I hadn't noticed the other Unseelie having animal characteristics besides wings, but her guard didn't have antlers. Maybe it was just some of them.

"Are you the Evil Eye?" I asked, wishing she was called anything else.

"Indeed, Heir of the Fae."

I twitched. "What did you call me?"

"Come closer."

"What did you call me?"

"*Come closer.*" The demand was so strong in her voice that I obeyed.

I walked to her and stopped in front of her. "How do you know me?"

"We all do, though many might not recognize you." She tilted her head to study me, her dark eyes glinting. "I've been expecting you for a while now."

"Why?"

"You have questions, do you not? About your heritage and your magic."

"You'd answer them?"

"For a price."

A woman after my own heart. "What do you want?"

"A bit of Blood Sorcery. You have magic that I do not."

That was true enough. "What kind of Blood Sorcery? I'm not going to do anything dark."

The woman cackled. "No, not your style, is it?"

I shrugged.

"I want a potion that will increase my powers. My ability to see wanes with time, but you can make me something to restore it."

"Probably, yes. Depending on what ingredients you have."

She gestured to her right, and I turned enough to see the vines retreat from the wall and reveal shelves full of potion-making ingredients.

"Impressive," I mused. "Probably something I can use there."

"And in return, I'll tell you what you want to know. Most of it, at least."

"Do you already know what I want to know?"

"Of course." Her smile was all knowing, and suddenly, I was irritated with her. Seers... They could really get on your nerves.

I wanted to get this over with.

Quickly, I moved to the shelves. I'd have to do this fast, and the potion wouldn't be terribly strong. I couldn't see any harm in making her vision powers a bit stronger, and there was no doubt I needed her help.

"The King of the Seelie is unwise to come here," she said.

"I want to know why your kind invaded my realm," he said.

I glanced at the seer in time to see her shrug. "That was the decision of the queen. I'm not privy to her thoughts, even if I tried to see them."

"Queen?" I asked. "Is there a king?"

"No. Long dead." She gave a dismissive snort.

"Didn't like him?"

"Never met him."

"Hmmmm." I focused on the task at hand, mixing ingredients in a silver bowl. It smoked and fizzed, smelling of honeysuckle and tree sap.

When it came time to add my black blood, I gave it only a drop. Just enough to improve the old seer's magic for a short while, but not forever. I didn't trust her, so no reason to make her more powerful than necessary.

Once my blood was mixed into the potion, I walked to the old seer and held the bowl out to her. "You'll have to add a drop of your blood."

She nodded and sliced her fingertip with one gnarled claw. I shuddered, vowing to take good care of my nails in old age. That was *not* a look I was interested in.

Her black blood dripped into the potion, and I nearly jumped at the sight. I'd known that Unseelie Fae blood was black, but seeing it from someone else was a whole different matter. I'd never seen anyone with blood like mine.

Fates, this was weird. A homeland I'd never imagined. A freaking creepy one.

I shook away the thought and stirred the potion, then decanted it into an empty vial.

"All done." I handed the potion to the seer, who smiled and took it. Then she slugged it down.

Her grin widened. "Excellent."

I was glad I'd made her the real deal if she was going to test it.

"Now I need to know how to harness the magic inside me. I can't get ahold of it."

"That's because you haven't completed the ritual that all Unseelie go through. Until you do, your magic will never be useful."

"What is the ritual?"

"You must go to the palace and enter the Sacred Pool of the Unseelie. Only there will you find the answer to your uncontrollable magic."

"*In* the palace?"

She nodded.

Damn it. "Where, precisely?"

"At the very bottom level. Submerge yourself entirely and pass the tests."

That sounded super fun.

"Do you really know nothing about the Unseelie attack on the Seelie kingdom?" I asked.

She shook her head, and I believed her. I could try to use my magic to force her to tell me, but she'd probably stop me before I could.

"Why did you call me Heir of the Fae?"

"That, I will not say." She spoke so firmly that I believed her. And it was something I could figure out later.

"Do you have any directions for exactly how to reach the pool or to get past castle guards?" Tarron asked.

"There is a grand ball tonight. If you are dressed appropriately and have an invitation, then you will be able to enter at will."

Dressed appropriately? Shit. "We don't know how the Unseelie Fae dress for a ball."

"I will help you, if you will make me another potion."

"Deal."

Twenty minutes later, I'd made a potion, and Tarron and I were outfitted in spectacular Unseelie finery. They might be evil bastards, but they knew how to dress.

Tarron wore a sleek black suit with fine midnight embroidery on the cuffs. The high collars complemented his new sharpened cheekbones, and though he was as handsome as the devil, I preferred the normal version of him.

As for me, I looked *spectacular.*

I hated that I liked it so much, but the ball gown that the seer had helped Tarron conjure for me was magnificent. Midnight black and made of fine lace, it plunged deep at the chest and rose as a high-pointed collar around my throat. Tight lace sleeves ended at points over my hands, and the skirt was ephemeral, almost made of smoke, and danced on the air as I moved. An obsidian dagger was tied to a decorative belt at my waist. I looked both severe and gorgeous, which was my style.

Tarron had had to conjure it because the Evil Eye had explained glamours would not work in the palace. The potions we'd taken to make us look Unseelie would keep working because they'd changed our faces. But a simple glamour was blocked by the castle's magic so it was harder to sneak in.

"The final touch." The seer handed me an invitation. "Make sure they don't look at the name, for you certainly don't look like me."

Crap. That wouldn't be easy. I took the invitation. "Thank you for the help."

She inclined her head. "Best of luck."

We left, heading quickly down the stairs. Tarron carried a bag with our old clothes, and I longed for my boots. This wouldn't be easy in heels, and I was a pro.

As we descended to the ground, there was more hustle and bustle behind the windows of the apartments, as if dinner were being put on or people were preparing for the ball.

It was oddly normal.

We reached the bottom of the stairs and arrived on the main road, which was still empty.

I turned to Tarron, catching his gaze on me. Heat flickered in his eyes.

"What?" I asked.

"You look magnificent." His voice was rough.

Warmth flowed through me.

He shifted closer, and I couldn't help but mimic his actions, drifting toward him until my chest was nearly pressed to his.

Despite the danger that hovered all around—perhaps because of it—desire spiked in my chest. There was something about him that drew me, even when I was unsure of him.

It was a heady magnetism that drew us together. He pulled me toward him, his lips swooping down toward mine. I leaned up on my toes and met his kiss dead-on, crushing my lips to his. Heat surged through me as his lips moved expertly on mine. His strong hands wrapped around my waist and pulled me toward him.

I moaned as my chest pressed full against his. Hard muscles cradled my softer curves, and I fell into the kiss. It was impossible to resist him. The attraction that sizzled between us was epic on a scale that I couldn't comprehend.

A faint sound of clattering hooves sounded in the distance, tearing me from the haze of want.

I pulled away from Tarron and turned, spotting an elaborate carriage coming our way.

A terrifying black horse with a gleaming coat and red eyes trotted toward us, pulling a sumptuous black carriage that was decorated with delicate carvings and gleaming midnight paint.

Swiftly, Tarron stepped around me and into the road, stopping the carriage in its tracks. The horse pulled up short, neighing, and I realized there was no driver.

Weird.

With the carriage stopped, Tarron stepped around to the side door of the carriage. Curtains were pulled so that we couldn't see inside, and he pulled open the door and climbed in.

There was a rustle of movement, and I spotted his fist flying.

Heck yeah, he was getting us a ride.

I climbed in after him, spotting two unconscious male Fae slumped on one of the bench seats. A golden lantern glowed on their slack faces as Tarron bound their hands and wrists with strips of their shirts that he'd torn off.

"Nice work. We needed a ride. No one just walks up to a fab ball in stilettos." I shut the carriage door behind me and rapped on the ceiling of the carriage. I had no idea if that would work, but it was what they'd done in a few historical romance novels I'd read.

The carriage rumbled forward as the horse picked up the pace.

We both ignored the fact that we'd just kissed as if we were a normal couple.

We were anything but a normal couple.

Not that the fated mate bond knew that.

"Do you think he knows to go to the ball?" I asked.

"I think so, given their attire." Tarron finished binding them and sat back on the bench seat next to me.

I tried not to focus on the heat of his thigh pressed to mine and turned to the window, drawing back the curtain to look out. It wasn't long before the carriage turned into the main city, rolling down long avenues paved in black stone. The buildings soared just as high here, fanciful structures out of a dark dream.

Overhead, the stars glinted ever brighter, and on the streets, people in finery spilled out of their houses. We reached the castle ten minutes later, passing by a guard house that looked more ceremonial than active.

"They aren't big on security here," I murmured.

"No, and the ease with which we've infiltrated makes me think that maybe we should increase security in our court."

"The Fae are known for their cockiness."

He inclined his head. "True enough. We're confident in the protected nature of our realms. Who would dare invade?"

"Me."

He huffed a slight laugh.

The carriage rolled to a stop, and we both stiffened.

Tarron moved to the door before it could be opened for

us, pushing it open into the night and climbing out. I followed, careful to shut the door behind me so no one could see the bodies inside. I left the bag of clothes, hoping we could find it later. I loved those boots.

Tarron tapped the side of the carriage, and the horse dragged it forward, off to wherever he would wait for his owners.

We stood in an elaborate courtyard at the front of the palace. The enormous structure was built of sparkling black stone that gleamed like diamonds. Huge windows glowed cold, crystal blue from lanterns within, and the building was ornate and delicate. I hated to admit that I really liked it.

Carriages and people milled around. Every woman was dressed in a fabulous black lace dress, and though they should have all looked the same, the variety was so great that it was a spectacle of Fae fashion. The men as well all looked different, each dressed as amazingly as the next.

Many of them had animal characteristics that the Seelie did not. Horns, strange eyes, claws. But for the most part, they looked human.

"Their wings," Tarron murmured.

Shit, he was right. Every Unseelie had their wings out. Clearly, it was a thing at formal balls.

Tarron's wings flared behind his back, powerful and gorgeous. Like lightning.

I drew in a steady breath and focused on what he'd taught me, calling my wings forth with great effort. Tarron touched his hand to my shoulder, and it helped me mimic his magic.

Once they were out, it felt strange. It was a strain to keep them flared behind me, but I managed as we joined the line of revelers that crept up the stairs toward the huge main doors.

As we stood in line, a few people looked at me strangely. As if they recognized me. I frowned, dipping my face down. No need to draw attention.

Attendants stood on either side of the main entry, taking invitations. My heart started to race a bit faster as we neared the one closest to us.

He had an eagle eye for the little pieces of paper that the partiers handed him, obviously reading each name.

As people approached attendants, they drew their wings back into their bodies. Probably because of the crush of Fae all around us. Gratefully, I withdrew mine into my body.

When we reached him, Tarron handed the invitation to the attendant, his thumb carefully covering the name.

The attendant yanked it out of his hand, peering closely at the little paper.

Shit.

10

THE ATTENDANT LOOKED UP AT US, A FROWN CREASING HIS pale brow. "You are not the Evil Eye."

Aaand, shit.

I couldn't try my suggestive magic on him. There were far too many witnesses, and the woman behind me watched like a hawk. I could just imagine telling her I was flicking a fly off his forehead.

Yeah, she wouldn't believe that.

And pulling a knife to threaten was a no-go. He'd shout and every Fae would be on us.

I leaned over, looking confused. "Oh, we must have picked up my aunt's invitation by mistake."

He frowned. "The noble seer has no relatives."

Aaand, double shit.

"My mistake." I smiled and grabbed Tarron's hand. "We'll be going."

Quickly, we strode through the crowd. Two guards

appeared behind us, ready to frog-march us out if we so much as balked.

This wasn't the plan.

We reached the bottom of the palace stairs, and each guard grabbed one of our arms. I glanced over at Tarron, and the sight was frankly ridiculous. He was far bigger than the guard, and still maintained the relaxed bearing of an all-powerful king.

He looked like he was letting the guy hold his arm as a favor.

Which, he kind of was.

My guard's black uniform was as stiff as his voice. "This way."

They turned us down a corridor that led past the side of the castle. It looked a bit like a service corridor, with the castle wall on one side and high hedges on the other. The castle windows were a good twenty feet above us, and I had a feeling we were walking along some kind of dungeon.

We were well out of sight and hearing of the crowd in front of the palace when Tarron and I met eyes. We nodded, then each of us stuck out a leg and tripped our guard.

Mine stumbled forward, and I whirled on him, punching him right in the nose. He reeled backward briefly, then righted himself and came at me. I ducked his right hook and hit him again, square in the middle of his face.

I gave it some extra Dragon Blood strength, and he

collapsed backward into the hedges, totally unconscious.

I shook my hand. "Haven't been in a fistfight in ages."

Tarron was already kneeling on the ground, reaching for his unconscious guard's embroidered belt, no doubt to bind his hands. "It's good for the soul."

I grinned at him. "Couldn't agree more."

I reached for my guard's feet and dragged him out of the bush, then mimicked Tarron's actions, binding my guard. Once they were bound and gagged, we shoved them deep into the hedges and straightened.

I brushed my hands off. "Ready to gatecrash?"

"Excellent idea." Tarron turned to the castle and looked up.

I followed his gaze, eying the smooth castle walls. They glittered black in the dim light, extending twenty feet up to the first window that was covered in crystal glass. Icy blue light gleamed from within. Delicate black roses climbed on thorny vines up the wall, but they weren't a great option for climbing. They'd tear my skin and my dress to shreds.

"Can you call on your wings?" he asked.

"I can try." I practiced what he'd taught me, managing to call them forth a bit quicker than last time.

But they weren't strong enough to carry me up.

Crap.

I looked at him. "No good."

He gestured me toward him. "Come here."

I moved closer as his wings flared wide behind him. He reached around my waist and pulled me toward him. I pressed full-length against the warm expanse of his muscles, and he lifted us into the air.

As we flew up, I called upon my Dragon Blood magic, slicing my finger and letting the black blood well. When we reached the glass of the enormous window, I swiped the blood across it for good measure and imagined it disappearing.

A moment later, there was nothing in front of us but air, and Tarron flew into the castle. We entered a huge hallway dotted with opulent silver lanterns and a rug that somehow managed to look like the night sky.

Tarron landed gracefully and set me down. I stepped back as he folded his wings into his body.

"Give me just a moment." I called upon my seeker sense, hoping it would draw me toward the sacred pool.

Nothing happened.

I tried again.

Nope.

I shook my head. "I'm getting a vague sense that it's that way." I pointed down the hall. "But not much more than that. My seeker sense is normally a bit weak, but the pool might also be protected."

"Likely protected. Come on."

We headed down the wide hall, moving quickly to avoid seeing anyone. At the end of the hall, there was an archway that led right into the front foyer of the palace.

There was a crush of Fae within, all mingling in their finery.

I looked at Tarron and raised a brow. "Perfect."

A small smile curved the corner of his mouth, and he nodded, proffering his arm.

I took it, and we strolled into the mass of people, quickly getting lost amongst the Fae. The main foyer was enormous, with a soaring ceiling and glittering chandeliers. Music trilled through the hall, something strange and haunting.

Midnight blue flowers bloomed along the walls, filling the place with the most amazing scent. Though many of the Unseelie had iffy-smelling magic because of their closeness to the dark arts, not all of it was bad. Something that I was continually noticing.

Tarron leaned down and whispered in my ear, making me shiver, "Some of them are looking at you as if you're familiar. Doing double takes."

"I know. It weirds me out."

"You have no idea why?"

"None." But I wanted to know.

The crowd was surging toward the exit, so we followed, eventually spilling out into a huge ballroom. A wide, sweeping staircase led down to a dance floor as big as a football field. Hundreds of Fae filled the space, dancing with a grace I'd never seen. The ceiling above was actually stars, open to the night sky.

The Unseelie were as nature-oriented as the Seelie, but in a darker way.

It was more beautiful than I'd expected.

My gaze lingered on certain faces in the crowd. Was my mother here?

I shook away the thought. There was no time to dwell on that.

"What are your plans for finding this pool if you can't get a good sense of its location?" Tarron asked.

"Not sure yet. Any idea how you're going to figure out why they invaded your domain?"

"Find the queen. Confront her if I have an opportunity. Spy if not."

I frowned. "Can you wait until I'm in the pool, at least?"

He nodded. "I'll escort you there. Once you're in, I'll go find her."

"Good." I had a great vantage point from the foyer at the top of the stairs, so I peered around the room, looking for an easy exit.

This place was so big, how would I even know I was going in the right direction? I could spend hours looking, and in that time, someone could discover the bodies in the carriage and realize that something was up. "I'm going to find someone to ask."

"Ask?" He raised a brow.

"Fine, enchant. Seduce. Beat the information out of. Whatever phrase you prefer." I spotted a likely looking guard in a corner, near a small door. He looked bored and annoyed. "Wait here."

Tarron found a spot near the wall while I drifted toward the guard. There were too many people on the landing where we stood. That was no good.

I sidled up to the guard and gave my voice a husky timbre. "Hello, handsome."

His eyes widened slightly.

"I'm a bit...bored here." I pursed my lips, going for a sultry frown, and ran my fingertip down the front of his jacket. "Are you?"

He frowned.

Okay, I was going to have to be more obvious. My tone of voice couldn't make it clearer what I was after, but he was pretty damned dense. I ran a finger down the expanse of skin at my chest, giving him a suggestive look. It was painfully obvious and over the top, but he was a fan from the look in his eyes.

"I have this little thing I like to do at balls, you see," I purred. "Start it off with a bang. And you look like just my type."

"Madam..." His cheeks flushed.

"Don't you have somewhere we could be alone?" I leaned up to whisper in his ear. "I promise to show you a good time. It'll be quick. You'll be back at your post in no time."

He cleared his throat, then opened the door behind him. I slipped through, cutting my fingertip as I went, and he followed.

As soon as he shut the door behind him, I whirled on him, raising a bloody finger to his brow.

But he was fast as a snake, smacking my hand down. "What's this?" he demanded angrily.

Okay, time for plan B.

I yanked a steel blade from the ether and pressed it

into his middle. He hissed in pain, the steel obviously burning him.

"Tell me where the Sacred Pool of the Unseelie is located."

His jaw dropped. "Why?"

"Tell me." I pressed the blade deeper, making sure that it broke skin.

He grimaced, his skin turning slightly green.

"I will gut you slowly," I said, making sure he could hear the relish in my voice.

"Fine, fine. It's in the deepest part of the castle. You can get there if you go through the ballroom and out the door at the end. Then follow the hall to the right, going down."

I peered hard at him, trying to determine if he was telling the truth. It was hard, so I pressed the blade deeper.

He gave a keening cry. "Fine! To the left. Go to the left."

"Ah, hiding the lie in with some truth. Smart." But I believed him now.

Except, what to do with him?

His magical signature was gross, for sure. Rotten cabbage, mostly. But it wasn't downright evil. Not so bad that I could kill him and know that I was ridding the world of true evil.

Though the Unseelie had invaded the Seelie realm...

Had this guy?

"Did you have anything to do with the invasion of the Seelie realm?" I demanded.

"The what?" The confusion in his eyes was genuine.

Okay, then. Only some Unseelie were aware of what the queen was plotting.

I pulled my blade away from his belly and flipped it around, then knocked him neatly on the head with the hilt. He collapsed, unconscious.

I stashed the dagger in the ether and pulled out his belt, then tied it around his wrists. His fancy tie—totally unlike anything in the human world, with its complicated knots and bows—went around his mouth. Then I dragged him into a corner and brushed off my hands.

A moment later, I sailed through the door onto the ballroom landing, acting like everything was normal. No one seemed to notice anything out of the ordinary, so I found Tarron and joined him.

"Well?" He raised a brow.

"Got directions. And also, not all of the Unseelie know about their incursion into your realm."

"So the queen is keeping it quiet."

"Seems like."

He nodded, his gaze thoughtful. "So perhaps the balance between Seelie and Unseelie isn't entirely broken."

"I thought you hated my kind."

"Only some of your kind."

"Hmmmm. We need to get to the other side of the ball-room." I turned to look at the dance floor down below. The whole thing was a twirling mass of bodies. If we wanted to get through, we were going to have to dance.

Fortunately, they were doing something like a waltz. I wasn't a bad dancer, thank fates.

I looked at Tarron. "Can you do that one?"

He scoffed. "Can I, King of the Seelie Fae, dance a simple waltz?"

"Okay, okay." I grabbed his hand. "Come on."

We descended the massive stairs to the ballroom floor, and I couldn't help but feel a *tiny* bit like Cinderella. Except I was always fabulous. No pumpkins for me.

When we reached the bottom, Tarron swept me expertly into his arms, one hand at my waist and the other gripping mine. I rested my free hand on his strong shoulder, and off we went.

Music soared as he twirled me around the room. For the merest moment, I was carried away by the romance of it. Stars sparkled overhead, and the air smelled of flowers with only the slightest undertone of dark magic.

Sure, I was hunting my probably evil mother and trying to save my town from utter destruction. Everything I loved was on the line.

But for this one moment, I was a princess at a ball.

And it was fantastic.

Tarron was an incredible dancer, effortless and graceful. I wasn't entirely familiar with the steps of whatever this was, but he kept me moving in a sublime rhythm that made me giddy.

By the time we reached the other end of the dance floor, I couldn't help the smile that stretched across my face. We slipped out of the moving crowd and into a stationary one.

"You're a good dancer." Tarron looked at me with respect.

Hmmmm. So that was what the Fae liked. Dancing and fighting. The two weren't that different, really.

"Not so bad yourself." I grinned at him.

There were about a hundred people on this side of the floor, all of them milling around and talking. Tables of food and drink were set up along the edges, and the delectable scent of the fruit wafted toward me.

I turned, unable to help myself.

Bowls of gleaming red and purple fruits sat piled onto the tables. Their skin gleamed like jewels, and the scent wrapped around my mind and drew me toward them.

I left Tarron without a word, walking toward the delicious offerings without a backward glance.

I just had to try one of them.

Doubt tugged at the corner of my mind.

Was that a good idea? Wasn't there something about Fae fruit? You weren't supposed to eat it unless you wanted to stay forever?

I couldn't quite remember.

A strong hand gripped my arm and tugged me to a stop right before I reached the bowls.

Annoyance surged in me as I turned.

Tarron frowned at me. "Don't."

"What? I'm hungry."

"You're not. That's Fae fruit, and it will force you to stay here forever if you eat it. You're a half blood, so it would likely work on you."

I recognized what he was saying—agreed, even—but it was damned hard to resist the pull.

"That can't be right." I tried to turn away, but he pulled me harder. "Let go!" I hissed.

He wrapped his arm around my waist and pulled me toward him, tucking me against his side as he dragged me away. I nearly reached out for the fruit, I was so desperate.

"You'll feel better when we get away from it," he said.

I grumbled, but my struggles eased the farther away we got.

Finally, we reached the huge doors that led from the ballroom and slipped through into a wide, quiet hall that was empty of people. As soon as the doors shut behind us, the pull on me ceased.

I sagged against Tarron's side. "Thanks."

He nodded. "It's all right."

"Why weren't you affected? You're not from this realm."

"I'm used to Fae fruit, and it's not so different from ours. You've never eaten it before. And it probably calls to you because it's the fruit of your people." As he said the last word, it was clear he was trying not to sound bothered by that fact. But he still was.

He trusted that I hadn't known I was Unseelie. But he still didn't like that I was.

Something shriveled inside me. I'd been forgetting our differences.

But they were still there.

As obvious as ever.

He was Seelie.

I was Unseelie.

My mother was involved with the invasion of his realm and the death of his brother.

And we were fated.

How the hell that was supposed to work, I had no idea.

"Let's go." I turned from him and started down the massive hall.

He caught up, but we didn't speak. Instead, we moved swiftly and silently across the deep red carpet. The windows were made of crystal that glinted almost blue beneath the sharp white lights hanging from elaborate silver chandeliers. It was a cold feeling—nothing nearly as nice as his castle.

So far, from what I'd seen here, there was a darker tone to the Unseelie world. But it wasn't explicitly evil. Sure, it had a tendency toward it. But it wasn't all bad.

I hoped.

Because this was my heritage.

Eventually, the hall diverged, and we took the left path. When it turned into stairs, we followed them down.

"So far, it's just as the guard said." My seeker sense even pulled me slightly forward.

The stairs flattened out into a hall, which was decorated with statues on either side. Various large beasts marched ahead toward another set of stairs that led downward. We were about twenty yards from the stairs when I stiffened.

"Do you feel that?" I murmured.

It was definitely magic of some kind, crawling across my skin as a warning.

Tarron nodded.

Right at the top of the stairs, two guards stepped out from behind statues. They each wore midnight blue uniforms decorated with minimal amounts of elegant black embroidery. Their eyes widened at the sight of us, huge and black in their pale faces.

"What are you doing here?" demanded one.

"Oh, we just got lost." I tried a little giggle.

He frowned. Clearly, he didn't buy it.

Yeah, I wasn't the giggling type, and it was probably obvious.

We kept walking forward, and I tensed, ready for whatever they might throw at us.

Both guards raised their hands, and neon green magic swirled around their palms. The stench hit me first.

Death.

I felt it next—cold on my skin.

No question. One hit with whatever that magic was, and we were dead.

11

———

THE GUARDS RAISED THEIR DEADLY MAGIC HIGHER, READY TO throw.

Hell, the Unseelie didn't mess around with this pool.

It was kill or be killed here.

A split-second later, the guards hurled their green death magic at us. It flew through the air, sparkling and bright.

Tarron dived right and I darted left, each of us slipping behind a statue before the magic hit us. The green death light plowed into the stone floor behind us, gouging it deeply and sending rock shards flying.

Thank fates I was fast and good in heels. It'd taken years of practice, but right now... Worth it.

I peeked out from behind the statues, spotting each guard raising another handful of green light.

"Damn, they're fast!" I hissed at Tarron.

Normally it took a little while for a mage to power up a

blast of their specific magic. But these guards weren't mages. They were Unseelie Fae, and they were deadly.

A blast of death magic hit the statue I hid behind, shattering it.

I ducked, shielding my face with my arms. Tiny pieces of rock sliced my bare skin, stinging sharply. At least I'd blend in with my black blood here.

I sprinted to the next statue for cover and drew my bow and arrow from the ether. It was my favorite long-distance weapon, and I was fast as hell with it.

Across the hall, Tarron was throwing fire at his attacker, using his elemental magic to swift effect.

I peeked out from behind the statue, firing off an arrow as the guard shot another blast at me. It plowed into the statute as the arrow sank into the guard's stomach.

He groaned and clutched at it, but only for a second. With a shaking arm, he raised another handful of magic and threw it at me. I sprinted out of the way, drawing another arrow and firing.

This time, it hit the guard in the throat. He tumbled backward down the stairs. The other guard took a direct hit of Tarron's flame to the chest. It was so powerful that it blasted him back until he fell down the stairs.

Tarron stood amongst the rubble on his side of the hall. A slice across his cheek revealed his red blood, but he was otherwise uninjured.

I hurried to him and gestured to his cheek. "Wipe that off and heal yourself. It's like a calling card."

He nodded but reached for me first, gripping my arm

and sending a surge of healing energy through me. The small cuts on my arms healed immediately, leaving me speckled with black blood that I didn't bother to wipe off. This was the only place where I'd fit in with it, anyway. First time in my life I didn't have to hide.

It was a weird feeling.

Nice, but weird.

Shit.

I didn't *want* to want to fit in here. That was crazy.

Tarron wiped away the red blood on his cheek and healed his own wound, then raised his hand. His magic surged, an autumn scent and the sound of wind whistling through the trees. All around us, the pieces of the broken stone floated into the air, drifting back to their respective statues and piecing themselves back together.

I looked at him, astonished. "You can turn back time?"

"No, manipulate stone. An elemental power."

"Handy." It might buy us some wiggle room if a Fae wandered by. They probably wouldn't even notice we'd come this way since it looked normal.

We hurried forward and started down the massive set of stairs that led deep underground. The guards' bodies were collapsed partway down, and we dragged them into one of the decorative alcoves that lined the staircase.

Down we went, deeper underground. The air grew cooler, and the stone walls echoed our footsteps back at us.

Something shimmered in the air ahead of us, and I stopped abruptly. Vines reached out from the walls, green and bright. One shot toward me and wrapped around my wrist.

Tarron drew his blade from the ether, then raised it to swing at the vine that had captured me.

"No!" I raised a hand. "It's an Aerlig vine." We used to use them to protect our own magical pool beneath our house. "It's reading my intentions. I have to convince it that they are pure. If we cut the vine, we'll never get past."

His gaze flicked to the thousands of vines that waved in the air in front of us, blocking our path.

"And don't try to use your Fae magic. They aren't like normal vines."

He nodded sharply. "I'll never be able to convince it my intentions aren't harmful."

No, he wouldn't. He wanted to kill the queen and be done with this mess.

"Go," I said. "Find the queen. Then I'll use my seeker sense to find you when I'm done at the pool."

His gaze met mine and lingered. Something flashed in his eyes—something more than a simple *see you later*—but I couldn't quite read it. And I needed to be putting all my mental energy toward convincing the Aerlig vines that I meant no harm.

He turned and left, taking the stairs three at a time.

For the briefest moment, worry flashed in my mind for him. He was one of the most powerful supernaturals I'd ever met—by far. But still, he was walking into enemy territory alone.

So was I, though.

And if I didn't start focusing, I wouldn't make it out.

I closed my eyes and concentrated on my goal. *Use the pool like a normal Unseelie and do no harm.*

The vine tightened on my arm. Another joined it, twisting around my ankle and squeezing. Nerves shortened my breath, and I kept repeating my goal, trying to shove pure, calm energy into the vines.

Finally, they retracted. In front of me, the barrier of twisted green plant life drew back, forming a tunnel, and I ran through as fast as I could. It was impossible not to think of my home, which had such a similar setup that it nearly gave me hives.

It was just a coincidence.

But still, it was weird.

I raced down the stairs, my stilettos clicking. They were annoying as hell to run in, even if I was amazingly competent, if I did say so myself. I yanked them off and carried them, the stone cold on my bare feet.

Three flights down, the stairs dead-ended into a solid stone wall. It was rough-hewn and ugly—unlike anything else in this eerie palace. Black handprints streaked across the surface, and I frowned.

Then it hit me.

"Blood." I grimaced as I sliced my palm against the obsidian blade that was still hooked to my delicate belt. Pain flared and I pressed the wound to the stone. The rock greedily sucked up the blood. For good measure, I envisioned my purpose here. My pure intentions.

Mostly pure.

After the hellish childhood I'd had, I was *really* good at compartmentalizing. So I shoved everything negative I'd ever thought about the Unseelie to the back of my mind and focused only on what I would do when I found the pool.

Finally, the stone wall disappeared, and I ran through.

A few minutes later, I reached the bottom of the stairs. I had to be a dozen stories underground at least, and the cavern was enormous. It soared overhead, at least seventy feet high. Glittering black crystal stalactites hung from the ceiling, piercing down like daggers. Light shined from within them, illuminating the room.

The pool itself was enormous, gleaming a dark midnight blue. It was equal parts inviting and terrifying.

The thorn wolf appeared at my side, pressing his strong body against my leg. My hand came to rest on his head. "Hey, buddy."

Bacon.

"I'd rather be eating that, too."

Instead, I was staring down my transition to full Unseelie Fae.

For a split-second, I didn't want to do it. I didn't want to be different. I was confident in my ability not to turn to evil.

Right?

Of course.

I'd been a Dragon Blood for all my life, able to access

the greatest amount of power in the world if I wanted. I'd resisted.

I would resist this, too. Whatever pull the Unseelie might have on me, I wouldn't cave.

But still, it made me nervous.

I shook the thoughts away and started forward. Burn walked all the way with me, his paws silent on the rock. He calmed my soul, our connection making me feel stronger. Braver. I reached the edge of the stone ledge and dropped my heels, staring out at the pool below.

I'd have to dive in. There would be no gradual wading.

I drew a deep breath, heartbeat thundering, and removed my hand from Burn's back.

"Here goes nothing."

I dived in.

Cold water closed around my head, magic pulling me deep. I made to swim to the surface, but something dragged at me. A powerful force yanked me down to the bottom of the pool.

Panic flared in my chest. I fought, trying to swim upward. But the magic here was too strong.

My lungs burned, about to burst. I resisted the desire to suck in air.

Until I couldn't.

The magic kept me pinned to the bottom of the pool for so long that eventually, my mouth opened, and I breathed in water. I could no longer control my own body.

Water filled my lungs and terror my soul. My heart beat so loudly that it nearly deafened me.

Holy fates, had this been a mistake?

I swirled through the water, consciousness fading. The current dragged me faster and faster, sucking me farther down.

Suddenly, I was falling through air. For the briefest second, I thought of my wings.

Then my descent slowed, and I landed softly on the ground.

I stumbled, then righted myself.

Strangely, I was dry. And I could breathe.

I sucked in the biggest breath ever. "Thank fates I'm not dead."

I stood in the middle of an enormous crystal room. The ceiling arched above me, with delicate filigree that opened to the night sky above. I turned, drawn by a sense of power and energy.

Behind me, a woman stood.

Well, not quite a woman.

She was more like a figure made of ephemeral black smoke. Power radiated from her, both dark and light. It was darker by far, but not all bad.

The essence of the Unseelie, perhaps.

Whatever she was, it was easy to read her. She was ruthlessness. Self-interest. Cunning. Cleverness.

I was all those things.

But there was goodness there, too. Albeit in small portions and buried deep down.

She moved toward me, floating on a faint breeze.

"Who are you?" I asked.

"That is not what you should be asking, Heir of the Fae."

"What?"

"You've come to complete your trials."

"Yes. But why did you call me Heir of the Fae?" She was the second person to call me that. The Evil Eye had done so as well.

"You will see. There is much you must learn here. Much you must do. But first, you have to master your magic."

Frustration buzzed within me. I didn't know if she was a seer, but she acted like one, speaking in their riddles and clues.

"Onward." She waved her hand, a broad, sweeping gesture.

The floor fell out from beneath me.

Suddenly, I was falling in earnest, plummeting toward the ground with wind tearing at my hair. My stomach leapt into my throat and I tried to scream, but no sound erupted. I couldn't see the ground below me or anything above.

I was just falling through space. No, I was being dragged toward something. A force pulled me downward, hard and inescapable. There was nothing to grab onto. Nothing to stop my fall.

Terror filled me.

Then I caught the scent.

Autumn.

The taste…honey.

And the touch. Like the caress of the ocean.

Tarron.

He was here.

My heart leapt. He was saving me.

Exhilaration and joy filled me.

But then I felt it. *Really* felt it.

His power was coming from down below, dragging me to him.

But I would die when I hit the bottom. I was going so fast, that was the only option. I was totally out of control. And it terrified me.

Out of control with him. Out of control with my magic and the great chasm that I'd created in Magic's Bend.

It'd been haunting me since I'd met him. Since my wings had appeared and my magic had gone haywire.

And now my fear was going to kill me.

No.

I wouldn't let it. I couldn't.

My thoughts flashed by in a millisecond. All of Magic's Bend was counting on me. I'd hoped to come here and be taught how to use my powers. Instead, they'd chucked me off a cliff, and I either had to make them work or I would smash to the rocks below.

Sick bastards.

I was being forced to get over my fear of my lack of control or literally die.

For the briefest second, I froze.

I couldn't help it.

Fear had made my wings come out before, but this was

so crippling that it froze me solid. Tarron's magic continued to pull me down, harder and harder.

No.

It took everything I had, but I forced my magic to the surface. I was done being afraid.

My wings flared from my back, and I shot upward. Tarron's magic continued to drag at me, and I flew as fast as I could, racing upward. Wind tore through my hair, and elation filled me.

The threat passed, and I flew into a calm night sky. My wings didn't falter even though the danger was gone.

The ground beckoned, and I landed gracefully in an empty meadow. I pulled my wings back into my body, and they disappeared effortlessly. For good measure, I called them back out, and they appeared immediately.

Finally, they felt like a part of me.

But I frowned.

That challenge had been so strange. Why had they used Tarron and his magic as the threat?

Was it just because he was emblematic of my fear of losing control?

Or was he actually important to me?

The Unseelie were totally fucked up in a lot of ways—I'd seen that for myself as I'd walked through the clouds of their magic. Perhaps it was just like them to use something important to me in a lesson that could kill me.

I shivered, turning in a circle.

The sight that caught my eye sent a frisson of fear straight through my heart.

Aeri, tied by the waist and hanging from a rope high above the ground.

"Aeri!" I sprinted for her.

She struggled, two hundred feet over the stone ground below. A flame shot across the sky, moving toward the rope that kept Aeri aloft.

It would hit the rope, and when it did, she would fall.

And die.

I knew it without a shadow of a doubt.

I tried to transport directly to her, but something about this place blocked that power.

It was going to force me to do it the hard way.

The terrain between her and me was crazy—arched stone bridges, strange stepping stones that created obstacle courses, pools of bubbling liquid that steamed.

No way I was going over all that.

I called upon my wings, ready to grab her. They appeared immediately, magic surging within me and flaring from my back. Ephemeral and silver, they carried me into the air when I launched myself upward. I flew toward Aeri, moving awkwardly but fast as hell.

Heat exploded against my back, pain and fire. It drove me from the sky, and I tumbled, unable to right myself as agony shot through me. I crashed to the stone ground, pain exploding in my shoulder.

Nearly blind with shock, I staggered upright, away from one of the bubbling pools of noxious liquid. My shoulder felt out of joint, and pain streaked down my arm. At my back, heat burned from the fireball that had smashed into me from behind. I spun around, finally spotting an Unseelie Fae.

He flew in the sky above me, his hand glowing with red flame. His dark brows lowered as he aimed for me again.

There was nowhere to hide. Though there were stone pillars jutting up from the ground about twenty yards away, I stood in the middle of a wide open space. I called on my shield from the ether.

But nothing came.

What the hell?

I tried again.

Nothing.

Something about this realm blocked the weapons I stored in the ether.

The mage hurled his flame at me. It shot through the sky so fast that I knew I wouldn't be able to dodge entirely. I braced for impact as I threw myself to the side.

It hit me anyway, pain flaring as the fire touched my skin. Then the magic seemed to soak into me, filling me up to bursting. It blasted back out of me, headed right at my airborne attacker.

The fire slammed into him, driving him to the ground. It was even bigger than it had been when he'd shot it at me, and he smashed to the stones in a flaming heap.

He didn't get up again.

I looked down at myself, shocked.

What the hell?

Aeri screamed.

I turned, heart pounding, and saw a blast of flame nearly hit the rope that held her suspended.

Shit!

I sprinted for her, then launched myself back into the air. My wings hurt from the flame that had blasted into them and my shoulder felt like an elephant had stepped on it, but I made it up into the air. I flew as fast as I could, wings aching and heart pounding.

When the cold pain sliced through my right wing, I screamed and fell, tumbling through the air. I hit the ground again, this time on my hip. Agony flared as I lay on the hard stone, stunned.

An icicle smashed into the ground next to my head, shattering in a hundred pieces.

Adrenaline drove me to my feet. I whirled, searching for the attacker. Another Unseelie stood on the ground about fifty yards from me. A black cloak whipped around her form, and her hair was tipped with blue. She grinned evilly and raised her hand, conjuring another icicle that could pierce me straight through.

Again, there was nowhere to hide. My shield wouldn't come when called.

I braced myself for impact, ready to dive. When the Fae shot the icicle at me, it flew through the air so fast I could hardly see it. I dived right, ready for impact because there was no way I would escape it entirely. These Fae were just too fast. When the icicle hit me, it didn't pierce the skin like it had pierced my wing. Instead, my body absorbed it and the magic that had created it. The power swelled inside me, then shot back out, an icicle forming in midair that hurtled right for my attacker.

She dived out of the way, barely escaping as the icicle whizzed past.

What the hell was going on with me?

12

I HAD A NEW POWER, BUT HOW THE HELL DID IT WORK?

My mind raced, going back over the three times I'd used this magic. What exactly had happened each time?

And then it came to me.

If I didn't see the blow coming, it would hit me like normal.

If I did see it and could brace for impact, I could send it back at my attacker.

Maybe I could even aim, if I tried hard enough.

The Fae called upon another icicle, aiming right for me. This time, when it flew, I stood stock still and stared at it. My heartbeat thundered so loudly that I thought it would deafen me, but I didn't try to run.

When the ice slammed into me, I let the power fill me up to bursting. I imagined sending it right back at the attacker's chest. A fraction of a second later, the magic exploded out of me and formed a gleaming blue icicle. It hurtled through the air and hit the attacker right in the chest.

She shrieked, then disappeared in a poof of smoke.

Maybe she'd been real. Maybe she'd been a figment of magic meant to force me to learn my skills.

Whatever the case, I had Aeri to save.

She was real. Not a figment. I could feel it.

I turned, my gaze going toward her just in time to see a blast of fire hit the rope that held her.

It ignited.

Terror flared in my chest.

The rope would burn, and she would die.

I nearly launched myself into the air, then stopped.

No. Just because I had wings didn't mean I should use them. I'd been too exposed up in the air. I needed to see the attacks that were coming, and when I was airborne, the Unseelie could attack from below as well as all sides.

I'd have to get right below her and shoot up from there, grabbing her before she fell.

I ran, sprinting across the stone ground. It arched up as a bridge ahead of me, and I followed it, crossing over a river that bubbled with acid. I tried to keep my gaze swiveling all around, searching for attackers.

Ahead of me, there were hundreds of flat pillars of rock jutting up at different heights. They looked a bit like the Giant's Causeway in Northern Ireland, and I could climb them like stairs if I was careful. They were all different levels, but I could run across them to the other side.

I raced for the stones, my injured hip aching and my

bare feet pounding on stone. I leapt onto the first stone, then the next and the next.

Something flashed out of the corner of my eye.

Bright light.

Electric current.

I dived low, tumbling on the pillars of stone but managing to avoid a direct hit. Electricity glanced off my thigh, hurting like hell but not keeping me down.

I scrambled up, whirling to face my attacker.

Another Unseelie Fae had climbed onto one of the stone pillars. His eyes glowed with the same electric blue fire that flickered around his hand. He hurled the magic at me, and I braced for impact.

It slammed into me, and I absorbed it, sending it right back at him. He dived left, freakishly fast.

Shit.

"You can't get me." He laughed, a sound so confident that I wanted to smack him in the face.

Again, he fired. I caught it like I had the last time, but when I sent it back, he dived away again, moving almost as quickly as the current itself.

The only time he stood still was when he fired at me.

Otherwise, he was *too* quick.

We could do this all day, except for the fact that every hit weakened me. Not a lot—not nearly as bad as taking a true hit. But it definitely depleted my power.

Subtly, I prepared to grab the obsidian dagger that hung from the decorative belt on my dress. This was a Fae fashion I could get behind.

As the Fae finally stood still to fire his magic at me, I grabbed the dagger and threw. My blade left my hand at the same time his electricity left his. He tried dodging, but I'd been too fast while he was standing still. The dagger hit him in the gut.

He stumbled, clutching the hilt of the blade.

I took his electric hit head-on, absorbing it and sending it right back at him.

Slowed by the blade in his gut, the electricity plowed into him, lighting him up like a firework. He dropped to the ground.

I turned from the Fae, spotting Aeri just as the flame ate through the last of the rope and it snapped.

I launched myself into the air, combining my Dragon Blood speed with my Fae wings. I shot like a bullet, reaching her right before she crashed into the ground. I grabbed her around the waist, and we tumbled through the air, finally slamming to the ground and skidding along the rock.

The dress tore, and it hurt like hell on my bare skin.

Finally, we rolled to a stop.

Panting, I pulled back, frantic. "Are you okay?"

Aeri was sprawled beneath me, looking pale and wind-blown. "Fine. Fates, that sucked."

"How'd you get here?" I demanded, not even sure where *here* was. It felt like a magical half realm. "Did they kidnap you?"

"Some weird smoke lady said I had to come help you

master your magic. She had power like I'd never felt." Awe echoed in her voice.

She had to be talking about the figure who had called me Heir of the Fae.

"And you just *did* it?" I nearly shrieked. "That's like getting in the car of a stranger with candy!"

"It was obvious she was telling the truth. I could *feel* it." She gripped my upper arms. "It was real, Mari. I mean, she's clearly kind of evil, but also immensely powerful. And you needed me. So I agreed, and some crazy magic swept me up and stuck me in that rope."

I threw my arms around her. "Jeez, you're dumb. But thank you. Let's get out of here."

She frowned, and her form seemed to shimmer. "I'm being pulled away." She drew back. "I think my part here is done. Good luck."

With that, she disappeared.

I stumbled back, shocked.

I felt like I was on acid.

Shaking, I stood and turned in a circle.

All around, the crazy rock formations disappeared. Wisps of smoke and mist began to fill the huge cavern. I spun, looking for a way out.

But there was just smoke. Some of it coalesced into big clouds low to the ground. They pulled at me.

I blinked.

What the hell?

Something pulled hard from my right, tugging at my very soul.

Truth.

I could feel it in my bones.

I turned to the right, squinting into the thick white mist. There was a figure ahead of me, shrouded in white fog and impossible to clearly see. There were more shadowy figures to my left and right. But only this one really called to me.

I ran to it, compelled by something I didn't understand. The word *truth* kept echoing in my head. As I neared the shadowy figure, the mist began to clear.

And I saw myself.

What the hell?

Another version of myself was running toward Burn, who was attacking an Unseelie Fae. The thorn wolf snapped at the Fae, his white teeth grabbing the Fae's arm as he waved a dagger.

"Burn!" I shouted.

The wolf didn't even notice me, just kept attacking the guard.

I looked at the other version of myself. She looked like hell, her lacy black dress torn, skin beat up, wings wounded from fire and ice. She was still running toward Burn.

"Hey, me!" I shouted, feeling crazy. "Mari!"

But the other version of me didn't look over.

I ran up to her, but she didn't so much as flinch when I tried to touch her shoulder. My hand passed right through.

This was a vision of some kind.

I spun in a circle, my head aching from trying to see

the other figures in the mist. Things were happening all around me, like hidden vignettes, but I couldn't quite see them.

I could feel them, though.

Some called to me, echoing with the word *truth.*

Others didn't interest me at all. *False.*

Hadn't Aethelred once mentioned his seer powers appearing to him in a similar way? Was that what was happening?

I needed to see more.

One shadowy figure pulled hardest at me, so I went toward it, running through the mist with my ragged dress flapping. Finally, the mist cleared enough, and I saw Burn again. Another version of him, attacking the same Unseelie Fae in the same way.

But there was no other version of me.

"Burn!" I shouted.

This time, the dog looked at me.

But there was still no other me.

Quickly, I darted toward Burn and touched his tail. Burn's thorns were cool and smooth beneath my hand, and the Fae he wrestled stared at me with anger.

I stumbled back, leaving them to their fight. They were definitely real, and definitely here. Burn had my back while I figured this stuff out, keeping the Unseelie off me to buy me some time to think.

My heart thundered and my mind spun.

I ran toward another group of figured.

When I got close enough that the mist cleared, I saw

me and Aeri. I was dressed as my usual fabulous self, whereas Aeri looked great in her sleek white silk suit. We both held wineglasses painted with vampire fangs, and we both grinned.

Hang on.

I'd bought those wineglasses last week, and we planned to use them during a *True Blood* marathon some-time in the future. We were saving them especially for that.

Was I really seeing the future?

I strode forward to the figures, who didn't so much as blink at me. My hand passed right through my other version's shoulder.

I played back the images of me and Burn in my mind. The first vision had been me witnessing the very near future—myself finding Burn in the mist, protecting me.

The second had not really been a vision at all. It had been me really coming upon Burn protecting me.

And now I was seeing something that should happen a week or two from now.

Holy fates, I *was* seeing the future.

I turned, spinning as I searched the mist for more visions. The figures who hovered just out of sight still echoed with feelings of true and false.

What if I ran toward a false one?

I tried it, heading toward a vision that didn't feel right. It almost made me nauseous to keep going, but I pushed onward.

When I finally reached the image and saw it, I nearly vomited.

Me, beheading Aeri with a sword as I grinned maliciously.

I spun away, my stomach heaving.

I would *never* do that.

That confirmed it—if I wanted to see the future, I just needed to choose to go towards the shadowy figures who felt true. I needed to control this. To ask the questions about things I wanted to see, not just be a passive vessel receiving messages from the universe about the future.

Tarron.

An image of him popped into my mind.

The feelings followed.

Confusion, sadness, admiration, fear, lust.

Fated mates.

What did that mean for us? What did our future hold? I was lying to him about my mother and the fact that her magic had been present when the Unseelie had invaded his realm—or at least, I was hiding the truth.

He hated my species.

Not to mention, he drove me insane. Insane with lust, and just plain insane sometimes.

We had so much stacked against us.

What did the future hold?

I couldn't help but want to cheat and see something. If one could really call it cheating.

Several of the shadowy vignettes called to me, but one of them screamed *truth.*

I ran for it, my heart beginning to pound. Adrenaline raced through my veins.

When the mist cleared enough that I could see the vision, I stumbled, confused.

In front of me, Tarron and I stood in a near embrace. Tears leaked in my eyes. Grief shined there as well.

And I stuck a dagger into his heart.

He fell.

Dead.

I stumbled back, gasping.

I would kill Tarron?

No. No way.

My head pounded. I ran from the vision, spinning and sprinting blindly into the mist. I ran until my lungs burned and my feet ached. Finally, I slowed, the white mist still floating around me, vignettes hazy in the distance.

I squeezed my eyes shut and shoved away the image of me killing Tarron. I couldn't think about that right now. I had to get through this.

It wasn't over yet. The mist would go away if this test was over.

I needed to ask another question. I needed to see something else.

Heir of the Fae.

What did it mean?

I needed a vision related to that. I called on my new magic. Premonition or whatever it was. It swelled inside me as the vignettes around me called out. One spoke particularly strongly to my soul, so I ran toward that.

My mother.

Heir had to do with my mother.

I needed to see her in the mist.

As I neared the vision and the smoke began to clear, my skin chilled with fear. What would she be like?

When I saw her, my eyes widened.

She looked just like me. Older, with thick streaks of white through her black hair, but just like me. No wonder some of the Unseelie had looked at me like they recognized me.

And for the briefest second, the sharpest desire pierced me. Desire for acceptance. From my mom.

A woman I'd never known who was probably evil.

I couldn't help it though.

My throat tightened as I looked at her. She wore a glorious gown of black lace and an obsidian crown that looked sharp and deadly.

A crown.

Queen of the Unseelie Fae.

Holy shit, my mother was queen.

Oh, that was *bad* news.

More figures appeared in the vignette as the scene changed. Tarron, bound with a thorny vine. Pain creased his features as the thorns stabbed him. My mother laughed.

My heart rate spiked, and I reached out.

No. He'd been captured.

Or he would *be* captured?

When in the future was this?

I couldn't see that.

In all of these visions, I'd never been able to tell when they happened.

But this vision—it would happen soon. Maybe in a few hours. Maybe in a few seconds. I could *feel* it.

I pulled myself away from the vignette, shoving it from my mind.

The mist cleared, disappearing as quickly as it had come.

Suddenly, I stood in the middle of the crystal palace again. The shadowy woman made of smoke drifted toward me on a light breeze. The same dark and light power radiated from her, heavy on the dark.

"You have seen, Heir of the Fae."

Thoughts raced. Aeri. My mother. Tarron.

"Is my sister safe?" I demanded. "Did you really return her to earth?"

"Didn't you just see her in a vision of the future?"

Oh, wow. She had a point. If I had been able to see her in the future, it meant she was all right. Adrenaline raced through me. For good measure, I tried again.

I closed my eyes and called on the power of premonition that had come to life inside me. Fog filled my mind, and if felt like I was back in the misty space I'd just escaped.

"Aeri. Show me Aeri in the future." I spoke the words aloud, not caring that I was talking to myself.

And suddenly, I saw her. Appearing through the mist, drinking a martini.

Truth.

My eyes popped open, and I searched for the ephemeral figure, knowing I had no time to waste. "Where's my mother? Where's Tarron?

She waved a smoky arm in a broad gesture, and the crystal ceiling of the palace disappeared. The dark sky beckoned from above. "Find them yourself."

She disappeared.

And I was done.

Somehow, I could tell that my trials were over.

I called upon my wings and launched myself into the air, flying up through the roof and into the night sky. Wind tore at my hair and ragged dress as I flew, shooting higher and higher upward. When the air turned to water, somehow I wasn't surprised.

I just started swimming, kicking myself to the surface.

My head broke through the water, and I gasped, my gaze going for the stone ledge where I'd first dived in. Burn stood there, eyes keen on me. He woofed low.

I swam for the edge and climbed out. My clothes were still ragged, torn up from my trials, but they dried in an instant. The high-heeled shoes sat where I'd left them on the ground, but I ignored them. There was no blending into the crowd now that I looked like hell.

This was *so* not me. I was currently a pumpkin and I did *not* like it.

I tried to give myself a glamour, but it didn't work.

Shit.

Just like the Evil Eye had warned.

"Come on, Burn. We've got to go find my mother."

He growled low in his throat.

"Shit, I was afraid of that."

Fates knew I didn't want her to be evil, but the signs weren't looking good.

For good measure, I tested drawing a blade from the ether. It worked, thank fates.

Gripping the blade in my hand so it was mostly hidden, I sprinted from the pool, racing up the stairs two at a time, my now-ragged dress making movement easier. I *loathed* being ill prepared like this and longed for the clothes I'd left in the bag in the carriage.

Just like at my home, the protections that had guarded the stairs on the way down had disappeared. I made it to the top in less than a minute, panting hard as I stepped into the wide hallway.

Burn followed, sticking right behind me the whole way.

I called upon my seeker sense, using it to find Tarron. It was easy, thank fates, and I headed in the direction that the magic pulled me. I tried to find my mother, the queen, but got nothing.

I'd find her soon enough.

As I ran, I passed Unseelie dressed in their finery. They gaped at me but did nothing to stop me. I still looked like an Unseelie from the potion, which wasn't a glamour, thank fates. It actually changed my face.

For all these Fae knew, I was just one of them having a really bad night.

Some were still looking at me like I was familiar. Because I reminded them of my mother. *Their queen.*

That was a head trip I hadn't been expecting.

A few of the palace guards frowned at me from their positions by the wall, but none stopped me. They looked at Burn, but did nothing.

Why?

When I reached the back of the castle where the art became more elaborate and the lighting fixtures more grand, I slowed.

I had to be reaching the queen's quarters, perhaps.

Oddly, there were no guards here.

The hair on my arms stood on end.

That was strange.

But I was nearing Tarron. I could feel it.

I tried to use my new prophecy gift to figure out what was happening with him.

It didn't work.

Damn.

Since I had no idea what I could be walking into, I slowed. Quietly, I crept toward a huge open arch that led to a wide spiral staircase. It had to go up to a tower. I climbed it on silent feet, seeing no one as I went. At one point, Burn disappeared.

A chill ran down my spine. This was too easy. I was about to turn back when I reached the door at the top. A cold voice filtered through.

My mother.

Somehow, I just knew. I had no memories of her, but I could sense it.

Unable to help myself, I paused, listening for more. As I stood, black smoke wrapped around me and froze me solid. It happened so fast I didn't even notice until my muscles felt tight and I couldn't use them.

The door swung open.

I struggled, trying to break the bonds, but it didn't work. When the mist picked me up and carried me through the doorway, my heartbeat thundered in my ears.

13

HOLY FATES. I'D NEVER SEEN MAGIC LIKE THIS.

It had come out of nowhere, picking me up like a rag doll.

This is how they'd caught Tarron.

Or how they would catch him, if it hadn't happened yet.

He'd never see this coming.

I struggled as it pulled me into the enormous round room, my feet floating over the ground. Fear chilled my skin. The ceiling soared high overhead, built of black tree branches that dripped with starry lights. A long table sat in the middle of the room, arranged with an elaborate silver place setting.

Though I thought I could feel Tarron, I couldn't see him. I prayed he was hiding and had the upper hand. But I didn't see how that could be, if this smoke was capable of so swiftly capturing an intruder.

A half-dozen Unseelie Fae stood around the room, all dressed in their finery. But I only had eyes for one woman.

My mother.

Blood pounded through my head, and my skin iced, growing even colder.

She stood at the other side of the table, dressed to kill. The ball gown was even more elaborate in person, the crown bigger and sharper. Her features were like cut glass, an Unseelie version of my own face. Though I probably looked even more like her because of the potion I'd taken. Her hair was swept up in an elaborate design that emphasized the black and white streaks.

I hated that I thought it was cool.

I also hated that I wanted her to like me.

It had been pretty much confirmed for me that my mother was evil. She had to have been the one who ordered the incursion into the Seelie realm and caused hundreds of deaths, including that of Tarron's brother.

But despite all of that, part of me still wanted her to like me.

Dumb.

"Daughter." My mother's voice echoed with an icy warmth, which should have been impossible.

"Release me," I demanded.

She smiled, and it was an eerie sight. "Come sit. Join me."

"Let me go."

The magical bindings loosened, but I still couldn't move.

"You look a wreck. Come, have some food." My mother gestured to the plates on the table, and they filled with fruit. Rich red wine filled the cut crystal goblets, glowing like blood.

Oddly, it looked good.

My stomach grumbled, then turned.

The magic carried me to the chair at the head of the table and forced me to sit.

My mother took the other seat, and the remaining Fae stayed standing.

"What do you want?" I demanded.

"Just some time with my daughter."

Oddly enough, I believed her. But it didn't sound like she wanted normal time. No. What she wanted was strange and wrong.

But how could it be so wrong if she was my mother?

I shook my head like a crazy person, startled at the insane thought.

Of course I wasn't on her side. That was nuts.

Something was getting into my mind. The magic that carried me, perhaps. Her influence?

Fates, I hoped that Tarron had some kind of genius plan, because I was in over my head here. My mind was growing foggier by the minute. Her magic. It had to be.

Before I lost my mind entirely, I needed info. If Tarron was hiding here, he could hear it.

"Why did you invade the realm of the Seelie Court?" I asked, wanting to get her talking. If I could distract her, maybe her powerful magic would fade.

"Why not?" She raised her brows. "I'd been captive so long that I needed a little excitement upon my release." She waved her hand dismissively. "Anyway, I'd like to expand the empire."

"Captive? By who?"

Her dark brows lowered. "Your father, of course."

"What?" I'd never met him either. Not that I remembered, at least.

"He didn't like the real me." She shrugged. "Said I was a bad mother. A dangerous one." She laughed. "Can you imagine?"

Yes, actually.

With the smoke of her power infiltrating my mind and making it foggy, I said nothing. I needed answers before I became too distracted, and starting a fight about her fitness for motherhood wouldn't get me them.

"So you escaped," I said. "And came back here."

"To my throne, of course. Your father is long dead, as he should be."

I'd suspected it, but it hurt to hear all the same. Apparently he hadn't been such a bad guy. And his poor taste in women meant that I'd been born, which I appreciated.

"So you tried to expand your empire into the Seelie Court," I said, trying to buy time until Burn or Tarron showed up to rescue me.

Nothing stuck in my craw worse than waiting to be rescued, but right now, my only weapon was words. Since I couldn't kill her with them, the best I could do was delay until help arrived.

"Precisely!" She smiled. "And it worked *so* well, too. Destabilize their people by turning their king mad! Even better, I forced him to kill his own subjects. Soon, chaos. It would have been mine for the taking, so easy."

My mother was a deranged psychopath. "Except we stopped you."

Her brows lowered. "Naughty girl."

I felt a flash of shame and regret over my actions in the Seelie Court. I never should have helped them. I should have helped my mother.

No.

That was her magic polluting my mind.

"And now you're after Magic's Bend," I said.

"No, silly." She laughed. "I'm after *you*."

"What?" Shock pierced me through the fog of her magic.

"I'll be honest, when you were a baby, you were a pathetic, whining thing. I didn't give you a moment's thought. Honestly, I'd have never thought of you again if you hadn't appeared in our realm to destroy the crystal obelisk. You were magnificent! Just like me."

"I'm *not* just like you."

"You will be." She smiled, and it was the scariest thing I'd ever seen.

Her words were the scariest I'd ever heard.

Because I *believed* them.

If I didn't get out of here soon, her magic would completely take over my mind. She was laying out her evil plan like a super villain in a bad movie because she was confident she had me in her grip. She wanted me to agree with her.

And I would. If I didn't get out of there soon, I *would.*

I struggled frantically against my magical bonds, but nothing happened. Literally *nothing.* I didn't so much as twitch.

Panic started to rise in my mind, but the fog of her power pushed it back.

Was this really such a bad place to be, after all?

My mother was so wise and powerful.

No.

"Why are you destroying Magic's Bend if all you want is me?"

"You'll have nothing to go back to, of course."

Oh fates. "The demon that I fought... He was sent by you, wasn't he?"

She turned to one of the Fae who stood to her left. "See? Isn't she so clever?"

He nodded, a sycophantic look in his eyes. Was he brainwashed, too?

Would I become like him?

I'd have shuddered if I could.

"But I created the crevasse," I said. "Our magic collided and created it when mine went out of control. How did you know that would happen?"

"You get your gift of prophecy from me. I knew you'd be there at that time and what would happen if I sent my demon to interrupt the one you were actually hunting. And voila!" She flourished her hands.

Horror expanded inside me. This was all so much bigger than I'd realized. I'd been fated to cause the horrible damage to Magic's Bend. I was like a disease that had been lurking in the city, waiting to strike.

Except...if my mother wanted Magic's Bend destroyed, surely it was a good thing?

No.

I could barely hold on to my own thoughts anymore. They came in flashes, followed by her polluting magic.

"But don't worry, dear. It will all be over soon. The crevasse is almost open wide enough, and the demons will crawl out and destroy Magic's Bend for good." She motioned as if she were brushing dirt off her hands. "It will be all gone."

Good. That would be good. Mother wanted it so.

Joy burst inside me, and vaguely, I felt the last of my consciousness fade. There was a pinch of grief, then nothing but joy.

Thank fates my mother had found me! I smiled at her. "That's good about Magic's Bend. I think I'd like to eat now."

The fruit beckoned from the plate in front of me, gleaming red and purple.

"Of course, my dear." My mother held up a finger. "But one little thing you must do first."

She stood and gestured to someone who stood behind me. I turned, spotting a man being dragged in, twisted thorns binding his arms to his upper body. Blood speckled where the thorns cut in, and he fought viciously to escape.

It didn't work. The thorns just dug deeper into his broad chest and strong arms. I couldn't see the color of the blood against his black clothes, but they gleamed wetly. A tiny bit of concern for him tingled at the back of my mind, but it was gone in a flash.

My gaze moved to his face. He was handsome. Devastatingly so. And familiar.

Ah, right.

He was Tarron, that Seelie king.

My mother would take his throne.

In the back of my head, I could almost hear a screaming sound. Like there was someone trapped in there.

"Dear?" My mother approached, holding out a blade. "You must kill him."

"Okay." I smiled and took the blade, then turned to Tarron. "You need to die."

His wide eyes met mine, horror flashing in them.

He fought, but my mother's magic reached out for him. I could see it now, wisps of black smoke. They wrapped around him and held him still. He could no longer fight against the thorny vines, but they'd done their work on him already.

I walked toward him, the screaming in my mind growing louder. I shook my head, trying to drive it away, but it wouldn't stop.

I sucked in a deep breath and forced it aside, stopping in front of the man and raising the blade high over my shoulder.

"Go on, dear. Do it." My mother's voice pushed my blade down toward the man's chest.

The screaming in my head grew so loud that it blinded me. Pain shot from my skull to every inch of my body, agony that made me curl over before I could push the blade into his skin. It tore me apart from the inside out, making me shake and sweat and freeze and burn.

I shuddered hard as my mind tore in two. There was a powerful popping sensation, a blast of hot pain, and then I was myself again.

I gasped, rising upright. My mother's influence was gone. Tarron stood in front of me, his eyes darting between the blade I clutched and my face.

My mother had released her magical bonds on me so I could stab Tarron. I whirled on her, raising the blade high and lunging for her.

She shrieked and lashed out with her hand, sending a blast of magic at me that I had no time to brace for.

It hit me in the face so hard that I flew backward, darkness sucking me in.

I woke in the dark, agony pounding through my head. Slowly, I moved my fingers—the only part of me that didn't ache.

There was dirt under my hands.

Panic flared, a cold sweat breaking out on my skin.

For a moment, I was back in Aunt's cell, a terrified

eight-year-old, all alone in a dark dungeon. A scream broke from my throat as I launched myself upward, head pounding with pain.

No. No. Get it together.

I was an adult. And I was locked in some kind of dungeon in the Unseelie Court. Memories of the past few hours flashed in my mind. I'd gotten control of my magic. I'd met my mother. I'd nearly murdered Tarron.

Who could be dead now, by my mother's hand.

My chest tightened painfully. I didn't want that.

Even though we were impossible fated mates, the last thing I wanted was for him to be dead.

Panting, I staggered upright. All of me hurt, but there was no time for that. I had to get the hell out of here and find Tarron.

So I did what I'd done hundreds of times in my life. I inspected my cell for an escape.

And like every time before, I found none. There wasn't even a door. Just a dirt box somewhere underground. They'd gotten me in here by magic, and I wondered if they'd ever bother to try to get me out again. I shoved away worries about running out of air and called on my magic.

But nothing happened.

No.

There was a powerful dampening spell on the place, enough that I had no magic at all. Not in here. There would be no transporting or using anything else to try to get out of here. Even my comms charm was blocked.

My heart beat so fast I thought I might pass out. This was how I'd felt as a child. Literally powerless in a cell.

I sat down on the ground and pressed my back to the wall, my breath heaving.

"Get it together, Mari." It was weird to talk to myself, but I had to. "You can do this."

There was too much riding on it. Vague memories of my mother mentioning demons spilling into Magic's Bend echoed in my mind. Memories of Tarron.

There was no time to waste.

"Burn," I called. "Burn, where are you?"

He was the only magic I had, and our connection was in our souls.

"Come on, Burn. You've got to find me." I pictured the thorn wolf in my mind, trying to build our connection. "Come on, Burn."

Something sparked within me.

Was that him?

I kept calling to him, feeling insane.

Finally, the dirt to the left of me began to bulge outward from the wall. It broke apart in pieces, and two thorny paws pushed through. Then a snout and a spikey head and two bright eyes.

"Burn!"

He shot out of the hole, and I jumped on him, hugging him tight. He pressed his thorns flat against his body to keep from poking me and licked my face.

The huge wolf had saved me.

I sat back on my butt and looked at him. "You dug all the way from the surface?"

Bacon.

"Well done, big guy. I'll definitely get you bacon." I looked around the room. "Can you find Tarron? Is he in a cell, too?"

Burn began to sniff around the room, finally picking a spot to dig. He went at it like a mad dog, spitting back dirt with his big paws. In moments, he'd dug several feet of a tunnel and disappeared inside.

I waited, since I'd just get hit in the face with the spoils of his labor. Tension tightened my skin as the seconds ticked past.

Please let Tarron be okay.

Finally, Burn appeared back through the tunnel, slipping out into the cell. There was a bit of blood around his mouth, but otherwise, he looked okay.

Tarron followed, bloodied and beaten and dirty but no longer wrapped in thorns.

Elation surged in my chest, and I dropped to my knees next to him. "Are you okay?"

"Yes." His eyes searched mine. "Are you?"

"Yeah." I was short of breath.

"Your dog got me out. They tossed me in a cell like this one, still wearing the thorn ropes. All of my magic was blocked. You've got a good dog."

I looked over at Burn, spotting his bloody mouth again.

"Oh, Burn." I had a feeling I knew how he'd gotten the

bloody mouth. "You'll be getting all the bacon you want, big guy."

He woofed low in his throat.

"Hopefully this will do for now." I dug into my pocket to retrieve a butterscotch and unwrapped it, then tossed the hard candy at Burn.

He leapt up and snagged it, chomping down happily.

I turned back to Tarron.

He was looking at me, the relief on his face replaced by confusion. Suspicion. "Your mother's signature... It was the same as the one that polluted my realm when the Unseelie invaded."

"Yes," I said slowly.

"Did you recognize it then?"

"Um." I hesitated, my skin growing cold.

"You did."

Shit. I should have confessed sooner.

"I could sense you were lying about something," he said. "Not about your magic, apparently. But about your mother's role."

"I'm sorry I lied. But I needed your help with Magic's Bend," I said. "I only recognized the scent. I've never been on my mother's side. But I didn't know how to tell you about it. Or when to tell you. You already didn't trust me. I didn't want to make it worse. I needed your help to save Magic's Bend."

"Telling me any time before now would have been good. Did you know she was the queen?"

I shook my head frantically. "I had no idea."

"Sure." He sounded as if didn't believe me. He shook his head slightly, mouth tight. "I can't believe we're fated mates."

"We shouldn't be! You hate my species."

"I don't." He scowled.

"Yes, you do."

"You lie too much."

He was right about that. There was nothing I could say to it. "I don't care about fate." That wasn't entirely true. But still. "I don't believe in fated mates. It's a Seelie thing."

"And Unseelie. And fate doesn't care what you believe."

"Well, fate is wrong, because we hate each other."

He gripped my arms, his expression intense. "I don't hate you. But I don't know that I'll ever trust you. But I can't resist you, *Mograh*."

Anger and longing flashed inside of me. This was a mess.

"This whole thing between us has me completely frustrated and out of my mind," he said.

"Well, it's mutual. And we have to get the hell out of here. I don't know what you heard from my mother, but there's going to be an attack on Magic's Bend soon. Demons will come out of the crevasse any minute. We need to close it."

He nodded and stood. "Let's follow your dog."

14

I STARTED AFTER BURN, WHO WAS HEADED TOWARD THE first tunnel he'd dug. He led us through a narrow pass that sloped upward toward the surface. It was close and tight, the walls feeling like they were closing in. The scent of wet earth filled my lungs, nearly suffocating me. I scrambled after the thorn wolf as fast as I could, desperate to get the hell out of there.

Finally, we reached the surface. I sucked in a deep breath of fresh air and scrambled toward some cover provided by a huge hedge. Tarron and Burn joined me, and I realized that we were in the same corridor next to the palace where we'd snuck in through the window. Apparently the dungeons were right beneath, which made some sense.

I reached for Tarron's hand and tried my transport magic.

Nothing happened.

No surprise, but it still sucked. "I tried my transport magic, but we're blocked."

"We have to get back to the portal. It will be the only exit, unless the queen has a private one."

"We're not going anywhere near her."

"Agreed. I've never seen magic like hers. It sneaks up and grabs you before you see it coming."

"Let's get back to the portal, then." I touched my fingertips to my comms charm. "Aeri? We're coming back."

"Hurry! Demons are starting to come out of the crevasse."

Shit. Just like my mother had said.

"Be there soon."

Tarron stood and stepped out from the hedges. I joined him.

Quietly, we crept along the corridor, sticking close to the shadows as we headed toward the back of the palace. There would be too many people out front still, and I couldn't blend in like this. We needed to get far enough away that I could use a glamour.

Finally, we reached the end of the lane and turned right through a small grove. Burn disappeared, off to wherever he went, and we crept through the fruit trees that called to me despite the knowledge that I should never eat them.

They were easier to resist, however, perhaps because I'd had practice with throwing off the chains of my mother's magic. She could control both mind and body, making her almost invincible.

Past the orchard, we found a collection of carriages.

"They must be waiting for the people from the ball." I searched for ours, hoping against hope. I spotted it and pointed. "Let's go get our clothes."

I raced over and pulled open the carriage door. The two Fae had regained consciousness, and they struggled against their bonds.

"Sorry, fellas." I grabbed the bag full of clothes and yanked it out, then shut the door again. "Someone will find you soon."

It was a shame we couldn't take the carriage, but I didn't know how to direct it, given that there was no driver.

I tossed Tarron his clothes and dug out my own, then went to the other side of the carriage and pulled them on. Finally, I felt like myself again. My clothes were my armor, and being so raggedly dressed felt gross. And since we were headed right back to battle, I didn't need to be making a pit stop at my house for clothes.

Dressed, I stepped out from behind the carriage. "Ready?"

Tarron was dressed in his black clothes again, looking handsome as the devil. The potion we'd taken to make us look Unseelie had faded, and I preferred his normal face.

"Let's get out of here." I turned and headed toward the edge of the property.

We hurried through the palace grounds, finally reaching the main town.

"Let's stick to the alleys," Tarron said.

I followed him through the narrow, winding alleys. At

one point, we were able to steal cloaks off a washing line, which helped us blend in even better.

As I made my way through the city, I realized how eerie it was to leave the darkness of the palace behind. Out here, we were amongst the regular Unseelie, and it wasn't quite what I expected. It was so much more...normal.

My mother's magic had clearly polluted the castle grounds and those within it—they were probably her main forces in her attempt to expand her empire—but out here, it was life as usual.

Sure, there was more dark magic and general trickery and mischievousness. Just like Darklane. But it wasn't all bad.

I'd have to think on this more.

Finally, we reached the edge of town. The meadow that separated us from the portal in the forest was completely empty except for the path that cut through it.

Tarron and I hovered in the shadows, watching.

"If the queen finds us missing, that road is the first place they'll check," he said.

"They'd see us right away. And the sky is completely clear, so flying isn't a great option." I peered around the edge of the building and looked at the main road. A wagon rumbled down it, the back piled high with barrels of stuff I couldn't identify. Two horses dragged it, but no driver. Just like our enchanted carriage from the ball. It was headed right for the path that led out of town. "I think I might see a possible ride."

Tarron turned to look. "Excellent."

The wagon neared, and I bent to grab a rock from the ground. The carriage was nearly to us, and the street was still empty. Good. Once the wagon had passed, I threw the rock in front of the wagon, and it rolled along the ground. The two horses rose up and neighed. The wagon stopped.

"Come on." I ran for the back.

Tarron and I climbed in between the barrels, and he conjured two rough brown blankets. We huddled beneath them, pressed side by side. His warmth seeped into me, both comforting and unnerving. We weren't exactly on great terms, but we had no choice but to remain together.

My heart thundered as I waited. Finally, the wagon began to roll. I grinned.

Perfect.

It was a silent, tense ride to the forest. By the time the shadows grew dark from the trees, I was ready to get the hell out.

"These barrels are full of potion bombs," Tarron murmured.

"What?"

He handed me one. "I just pulled it out of that one."

I looked at the low barrel he was pointing to, then at the small glass globe I held. A shining green liquid gleamed within.

"Shit." My mind raced. There has to be thousands of potion bombs in here. Enough for a huge attack.

If this was headed to the portal, that meant it was headed to earth. Probably to Magic's Bend. "Aeri said demons were starting to come out of the crevasse. I bet the Fae will be the second line of attack."

"We need to destroy this cart."

"Agreed." We were nearly to the clearing. "Let's do it now."

He nodded and climbed gracefully from the cart. I followed, sprinting to the front of the carriage and drawing a blade as I ran. I sliced the harnesses off the horses and smacked each on the butt. They sprinted off. When I was far enough away, Tarron hurled a fireball at the wagon.

It went up like a mushroom cloud, the explosion hurling me backward. I slammed into a tree and grunted.

Tarron ran toward me. "Are you all right?"

"Fine. I guess I was still too close." I staggered upright, my ears picking up the sound of footsteps. "Someone is coming. Hide."

We ducked behind a huge tree trunk just as a troop of Fae soldiers came. They'd run from the direction of the portal. No doubt they were headed to Magic's Bend.

"I'll take care of them." Tarron raised his hands, his magic swelling on the air, bringing with it the scent of autumn and the feel of water.

The earth rose up behind the Fae soldiers, breaking apart as Tarron forced it upward. The soldiers never even saw—they were too busy staring at the explosion. It crashed down on them, smashing them to the ground.

Groans sounded from beneath the piles of dirt, but it'd take them some time to dig themselves out.

"Let's go." I sprinted from my place behind the tree, headed for the portal.

It was unguarded, thank fates. Every single Unseelie had been drawn by the explosion.

I hurtled through the gleaming black portal, not even waiting for Tarron. He followed close behind, and we both arrived back at the top of Mount Schiehallion in seconds.

Cold wind whipped across the peak and chilled my skin.

I touched my comms charm. "Aeri, where are you?"

"Top of the big building on the west side of the street. The old music hall."

"Be there in a sec." I reached for Tarron's hand. As soon as his stronger one gripped mine, I called upon my magic, transporting us back to Magic's Bend.

We arrived in chaos. The flat roof of the old music hall was covered with supernaturals prepping for battle. Mages, shifters, and even a few city Fae. I caught sight of a few demon slayers I recognized from work, along with members of the Order of the Magica. They grabbed weapons and raced to the edge of the roof, jumping and climbing down to the street.

I ran to the edge and looked down. The crevasse was enormous. Demons climbed out, dozens of them. Our side fought valiantly, trying to hold them back with magic and might. Colorful blasts flew through the air as spells were cast and weapons flew.

To my right, Claire and her brother, Connor, hurled potion bombs down at the attackers. In addition to making a mean latte, Connor was a master potion maker. His sister, Claire, was a mercenary, and together, they made a mean team. Acid bombs and freezing potions splashed against demons, who shrieked and flailed.

"You're here just in time for the fun!" Claire shouted.

"Wouldn't want to miss it." Especially since I'd caused it.

Right beneath us, I spotted the shimmery blue form of Del, one of the FireSouls and Cass's sister. She was part phantom, able to adopt the form at will, and she fought like a mad woman, beheading demons with her sword almost as soon as they reached her.

"Mari!" Aeri's voice called from the right, and I looked over.

She sprinted toward me, dressed in her white ghost suit. Behind her, I spotted Cass. Her red hair gleamed in the early morning light. Magic swirled around her, and she turned into an enormous griffon. Gleaming golden feathers surrounded an enormous beak. Her sister Nix jumped onto her back, and Cass raced for the edge of the building, her huge wings carrying her high into the air. Nix also favored a bow and arrow, and she fired it expertly down at the demons below.

Badass.

Aeri reached me. "Are you okay?"

"Fine. I need to get down to the crevasse." I glanced at Tarron, who had stuck by my side. "Him, too."

"Let's go. I'll watch your backs while you work."

"Thanks."

"We'll keep an eye on you, too," Connor said.

"Thanks, guys." It would really help to have them providing top cover.

Aeri leapt over the side of the building and scaled down it to the ground at record speed.

"Let's do this." Tarron's wings flared wide, and he flew to the ground.

I followed, landing silently next to Aeri. We needed to reach the edge of the crevasse, which was only fifteen yards away.

Problem was, there were at least a dozen demons between us and our goal.

I looked at her. "Let's clear a path. Quick."

She nodded, immediately understanding.

We each drew a dagger from the ether. I sliced it against my palm, hissing at the pain. But I enjoyed it all the same. Anything to know I was in control.

I called upon the lightning deep inside me, stepping away from Aeri so there was a good twenty feet of space between us. She did the same, and we held out our hands so our palms faced each other.

"Now!" I let the magic burst out of me, the electric current lighting up my nerve endings with power and light.

The lightning shot toward Aeri, and her current joined with my own, creating a steady line of deadly force. This was a power I could only use with her, because we'd once created it together in an attempt to escape Aunt. It was badass, though.

We ran forward, dragging the lightning through any demon that stood between us and the crevasse. They dropped like stones, shaking and spitting.

Fifteen down.

We reached the edge of the crevasse, and I dropped my hand, cutting the electric current. I leaned over to look down into the darkness. My mother's magic welled up, along with the burning rubber smell of the demons and their underworld.

Whether she'd hired them as mercenaries or made some kind of pact with them, she'd gotten a great deal. There were hundreds climbing up the walls from deep within. All different species, but mostly fire demons from the look of the dark red skin and blunt horns.

"Fates," Tarron said from behind me. "I've never seen anything like this."

"I think it's a first." Normally, demons came through portals created by mages who wanted to use their services on earth. Their services being mainly killing.

This, though...

It was unprecedented.

All to get to me.

I shivered.

This was the *wrong* kind of motherly love.

"I've got your back," Aeri said. "Now get to work."

I nodded, drawing in a deep breath and calling upon my magic. It was hard to focus with the battle raging all around. To my right, Cass swooped low and bit a demon in half with her enormous beak. Behind me, I could hear

Aeri fighting another demon. Colorful blasts of potion bombs exploded all around.

"I'll start closing the earth back up as soon as you remove the magic that keeps it apart," Tarron said.

"Okay. I'll work fast." I forced the distractions to the back of my mind, focusing on the deep crevasse. Specifically, focusing on the dark magic that seemed to coat the thing. Now that my magic rested easily inside of me, it was like I could see for the first time.

Faint, glowing patterns covered the walls of the crevasse. They swirled over the surface, imbuing the stone with strength.

It was my magic. Or at least, it was the damage that I'd done. I needed to remove the magic swirls so Tarron could close up the ground. I had no idea how to do that, so I did what I always did.

I winged it.

I reached out with my power, trying to make a connection with the magic that I'd left staining the stone. It took a few tries, but I finally got ahold of it. If I removed the magic from the stone walls, where the hell would I put it?

I tried absorbing it back into myself, and it seemed to work. The magic flowing into my body made me vibrate with power, but I didn't stop.

It was so damned difficult, though. I felt like I'd lose the thread of it any moment.

As I worked, demons climbed the walls toward me. Tarron hit them with blasts of sunlight, making them tumble back down into the depths of the earth. They howled as they fell, the sound making my hair stand on end.

We worked together, magic joining in the air. The glowing swirls disappeared from the steep walls as I worked, drawing back into my body.

"Are you all right?" Tarron asked.

He could tell I was struggling. Exhaustion pulled at me. I gasped my response. "I'm fine."

I was going to need a *lot* more practice. If I managed this, it would be a miracle.

Finally, I'd gotten all of them. It just looked like normal stone as far as the eye could see.

I glanced at Tarron. "Try your bit. I'll hold the demons off."

Tarron got to work, his magic filling the air. I drew my bow and arrow from the ether, firing quickly down into the pit. This was so much easier than using my new magic. I aimed for the closest demons, hitting them right in the head. A few flew out of the crevasse, and I diverted my arrows toward them when they got too close.

"It's not working," Tarron grunted. "There's still more of your magic in the crevasse."

"Deep down." I stared into the darkness. Shit. "It has to be."

"Can you reach it?"

"No, I thought I got it all." I glanced back at my wings, which still flared behind me, silvery and bright. "I'm going to try flying in so that I can work from there."

"I'll be right beside you."

I turned back and shouted at Aeri, "I'm going in!"

"You better come back, or I'm going to kill you!"

"Fair enough!" I gave her one last look as she slammed her mace into a demon's skull, then I leapt into the crevasse.

My wings picked me up, and I soared gracefully toward the center of the space, then downward. The deeper I got, the more the magic reeked. I shivered, hating the feel of the darkness. We were about seventy feet down when I spotted my magic again. There was a lot more down here, damn it.

Yeah, I was going to need practice with this.

Tarron flew alongside, guarding me. The heat of battle had caused him to shift. His eyes were black and his silver horns curved back around his skull.

I got to work, reaching out with my power to remove it from the walls and draw it back into me. Exhaustion pulled at me, but I forced it aside.

Tension tightened my skin. "Something is coming."

"I feel it," Tarron said. He flew next to me, his expression intense.

A horde of flying demons hurtled up from down below, no doubt drawn by our presence.

I kept up with my magic, but I watched the demons intently, bracing myself.

One of them let a red fireball glow in his hand. He hurled it at me. I stared right at it, bracing myself.

"Mari! Look out!"

The fireball slammed into me right after Tarron's

shout. I absorbed the power and sent it right back at the demon who'd thrown it. The ball of flame smashed into him, sending him falling back into the pit.

"What the hell is that?" Tarron asked, throwing a blast of sunlight at one of the closest flying demons.

"New power. If I can see the hit coming, I can send it right back."

"I'll guard your back, then."

"Thanks."

As he watched my back, I kept my gaze on the demons coming up from down below. As I worked to wipe this place clean of my magic, I fought them off with my new power, sending back icicles, fireballs, and electricity.

Several times, I took a direct hit, unable to send it back. Multitasking with my new powers was nearly killing me. Every inch of my body ached, and my power was flagging.

But finally, I was nearly done. Just a bit more glowed from down below, calling to me.

"I'll be right back."

"Be careful!" Tarron was caught in a fight with three demons, unable to follow. He hit the closest one with a blast of sunlight, lighting him up like a firework. He could take care of the rest.

I flew deeper into the crevasse, called by the magic. I was out of sight of Tarron when the air started to feel strange.

My skin chilled.

What was going on?

Squinting, I searched the area around me for anything

out of the ordinary. There were some demons climbing on the walls, so determined to reach the surface that they ignored me. But there was none of my magic.

I *had* gotten it all.

So what had called to me?

"Daughter."

I stiffened.

Shit.

Fast as I could, I turned. I had to see her before she hit me with her crazy mind/body control magic.

My mother floated in the air about twenty yards from me. She was dressed in the most incredible leather fight suit I'd ever seen. Tight and covered in detailed embroidery, it was gorgeous. The high collar was severe in the best way possible, and her hair was swept up on her head in a ponytail that was streaked white and black.

I hated that I thought she looked great.

Because she also looked super evil. The light of it glowed in her eyes, and flowed with the stench of her magic. Putrid night lilies and brimstone.

Signatures never lied, and hers was downright disgusting.

Her magic flowed toward me, the black wisps moving fast.

15

As my mother's magic drifted toward me, I braced myself.

Please don't fail me now.

The dark wisps reached my skin, absorbing into me. She smiled, cold and hard.

Tension tightened my skin in the half-second I waited to see if my power would work against hers. When the energy filled me up, hope surged. I barely had a handle on it, but I kept it under control.

I moved my fingertips, just enough that I would know if my power was working but not enough that she could tell. I wanted the element of surprise on my side.

When my fingers twitched, I nearly grinned.

I resisted, demanding, "Release me!"

"Now, now. Why would I do that?" She frowned. "I don't think I will."

More of her magic flowed into me, and I absorbed it,

getting ready to send it back at her. I wouldn't have long before it burst out of me.

"What's happening?" I asked, trying to make my voice sound confused. Like I was being won over to her side. I wanted information anyway. "Who are the demons?"

"Just my minions." She frowned at me, tilting her head.

Shit, she could tell I was acting.

"What are you doing?" she asked. "I sense something different about you."

Like your magic can't control me?

I could barely control it myself. Her power filled me up to bursting. I had to release it soon. In one massive blast, I let it explode out of me. The gray wisps of smoke shot right back at her. With my magic, I reached out, trying to control them. I wanted to be able to control her like she had me. To bind her up and take her prisoner. Force her to call off the demons.

The gray magic shot into her, and she stiffened. "What's going on?"

"New power." I imagined her being perfectly still, bound just like I had been.

Her face turned red, and she twitched.

I smiled at her. "Are you struggling against the invisible bonds?"

She just grunted, rage flashing in her eyes.

"Sucks, huh?" I kind of liked turning the tables, even if it was draining the strength from me.

She turned redder, her rage flaring bright. And her magic.

Oh shit.

I'd definitely underestimated her power.

While she was bound, I drew my bow and arrow from the ether. Something sharp pinged in my chest. I couldn't help it.

She was still my mother.

But I drew back on the arrow and aimed, right for her chest.

"You bitch," she hissed.

"Runs in the family." I released the arrow.

It flew through the air, headed straight for her.

Right before it hit her, there was a massive burst of energy that slammed me backward.

She disappeared, transported elsewhere.

Shit!

I'd lost her.

And she'd definitely be coming back.

The sound of the battle from up above drew me. I had a job to do.

Since I had removed all of the magic from the crevasse, I flew upward as fast as I could. From below, I spotted Tarron. He wrestled in midair with an enormous winged demon. The creature's muscles were huge, but Tarron was just as strong. He got a blade between the demon's ribs, then kicked him away. As the demon struggled to pull out the dagger, Tarron hit him with a fireball, sending him blasting back into the crevasse. All around, demons howled.

"Try your magic now!" I shouted.

"On it." He hovered in midair, right in the middle of the crevasse.

As his magic swelled, I watched his back, raising my bow and arrow at any demon who flew near. I aimed for the heads, sending them hurtling into the pit.

Anytime magic flew at me or Tarron, I made sure to intercept it, absorbing the power and sending it right back at the attacker.

When a fireball hit my leg from behind, I screamed.

"Are you all right?" Tarron shouted.

"Keep working!" I beat the flames away, then whirled to face the attacker. Another fireball was flying right at me.

I braced, absorbing the power and sending it back. The fire slammed into the demon's head, and he smashed into a demon climbing the wall, and they both tumbled into the pit.

My leg ached as I flew, looking for the next attacker. I deflected more fire and a smoke bomb, but missed an icicle that left a deep gash in my bicep. I sent another icepick through the eye of the one who had thrown it, though, so I considered it even.

I was definitely running out of strength though. We needed to end this.

"Mari!" Tarron shouted. "Get over here!"

I flew toward him. "What's wrong?"

"This crevasse has become too deep. Too wide. Even I can't close the whole thing."

"What?!"

"It's not just the size. You created this, so your magic

will have to be present to fix it. You're going to have to help."

"I don't have any earth magic."

"You're a Fae. Find it."

"I *really* don't think I have it." An idea popped into my head. "But I could make it."

"Do it quick. Demons are coming."

I could hear the flap of their wings. The shrieks. There would be a *lot* of them.

"Okay." Quickly, I sliced my finger. Blood welled and pain flared. I imagined myself controlling the earth. Pulling the sides of the crevasse back together.

From down below, the demons neared. I could see them now, their massive bodies rising toward me.

"Faster!" Tarron's magic held strong as he worked to drag the earth back together.

"I'm trying!" Finally, I sensed it. The stone walls around me felt like they were part of me, and I worked to pull them together. Sweat broke out on my brow.

The demons were so close I could see the whites of their eyes. Too many to fight while also using my magic like this. Fear chilled my skin.

"Almost there!" Tarron shouted. "Get ready to fly. Fast!"

I could feel it. It was like our magic was reaching the tipping point. We were pulling on the earth, and soon, the two sides of the crevasse would snap back together.

The earth rumbled, a deep groaning noise that shook my bones. I looked down, spotting the earth closing back up.

Shit.

It moved so fast that my head spun. The stone walls crushed the demons who were right below us. I shot upward, flying as fast as I could. I dropped my bow and arrow, needing to be as aerodynamic as possible. From below, the earth closed, flattening the rest of the demons who still climbed the walls. Tarron flew alongside me, his powerful wings carrying him fast.

I gave it my all, lungs heaving and muscles aching. Finally, I shot out of the crevasse and into the sky. Beneath me, the earth snapped back together, the force making all the fighters go to their knees.

An ugly scar ran down the street, but the west end of Magic's Bend was back together. Roughly two dozen demons were still alive on the surface. They climbed to their feet. The citizens of Magic's Bend attacked fast. Weapons and magic flew, felling the demons almost as quickly as they stood. Now that the monsters weren't spilling out of the crevasse at record speed, they were able to take out the rest in seconds.

Panting, I lowered myself to the ground, landing in an empty, shadowy alley. I could see the main street where the battle wound down, but it was quiet here. Tarron followed, landing next to me. He was disheveled and covered in burn marks and wounds. The demons had gotten in a few good hits. On me, too, actually. My leg and arm ached like hell, and I wouldn't be able to walk right for days.

All around, the fighting faded. The wounded tended to

each other. I could see Aeri, who looked beat-up but fine. The FireSouls and Connor and Claire, too. Other Demon Slayers, here to clean up my mess.

What kind of thank you present did one buy for this kind of work scenario?

There probably wasn't one.

"Are you all right?" Tarron's voice was rough.

"Yeah, you?"

"Fine." He reached for me and gently gripped my arm. As his healing magic flowed into me, the pain began to fade.

What the hell was going on with us?

He healed me first, but he hated what I was.

As the pain faded, pleasure took its place. There was no way to resist it. I just felt this way around him. Any time he touched me, I lost my mind.

Whether it was fate or my own body, I didn't care.

His eyes darkened as he leaned nearer, clearly feeling the same thing.

All around, the chaos faded away. It was like we were in a bubble, here in the empty alley.

Tension tightened the air between us, drawing us irresistibly together. The heat of the battle, the fear. The danger. All of it drove my desire higher.

I couldn't fight it.

So I didn't try.

Desire pushed me toward him. He moved toward me, as well. We collided together, our lips finding each other's in a crushing kiss. His strong arms wrapped around my waist, and I threw my own around his neck. He dragged me against the hardness of his chest, and I moaned. He felt so powerful under my hands.

His lips ravaged my own, making pleasure surge through my body. It tightened within me, lighting up all my nerve endings. I parted my lips, and his tongue dipped inside my mouth. He was an expert kisser, making my head spin.

The scent of his magic and his desire wrapped around me as he held me tight against his heat. I plunged my hands into his silky hair, wanting to run my mouth over every inch of his body.

Not here.

The thought snapped me into reality.

We had just finished a battle. There were wounded just a few yards away.

Shit.

I pulled back. He groaned, but released me.

I stepped away from him, breaking all contact. Cool air kissed my skin, bringing me back to my senses. "We shouldn't have done that."

"I can't seem to help myself."

"You would if you could, wouldn't you?" The idea hurt.

"We're fated."

"I don't think I want to be." I shoved my fingers through my hair, frustrated. "You drive me insane, yet fate decrees that we should be together? Why is it so difficult?"

"*Mograh* doesn't mean instant love."

"It sure as hell doesn't."

"It just means that we're drawn together. That something about our souls just fit."

"I don't feel it."

"Really?" He gave me a knowing look.

I scowled. But he was right. We *did* just fit. Despite the fact that we were always at odds and didn't trust each other. He couldn't trust me after I'd lied so many times, and I couldn't trust that he actually cared and wasn't just hanging around to get vengeance for his brother.

But I always knew where he was. I was always there to protect him. Driven to do it. Just like he was driven to protect me. He'd probably saved my life a half dozen times in that crevasse, and vice versa.

And no matter what, I was drawn to him like a magnet.

I felt good around him, even when I was pissed.

And we couldn't stop the desire that flared between us.

"I don't want to think about this right now," I said, my gaze going to the chaos out in the street. I needed to get out there to help. "There's still a mess to be cleaned up."

He nodded sharply. "First, what happened down in the crevasse? The magic felt strange."

For the briefest moment, I debated telling him. Then I spat the words out, not wanting to hide things like I had before. "My mother was down there."

"Coming to the surface?"

"Coming to get me. She tried to use her controlling magic again." Of course my mother had the magic that I feared the most. I hated being out of control, so that's what she did.

"It didn't work, though."

"No, I managed to use it against her. I almost got her, too. Arrow right to the heart. But she disappeared."

"Where?"

"Portal. Probably back to the Unseelie Court."

"She won't stop."

"No, she won't."

"I'll help you." He shrugged very slightly. "Which I admit, is also helping me."

"You want vengeance." I knew it was the main reason he had helped me.

He grinned savagely. "Desperately."

"You'll have it." Because I needed to defeat her, and together, we had our best shot.

This meant we'd be working together to find her. Probably falling more for each other, since we couldn't seem to help it.

I stepped aside. "I'll see you later. I've got to go clean this up."

As I walked past him, he grabbed my arm gently. "I believe you didn't know about your mother. That she was queen, I mean."

I looked back at him. "Good. Thank you. I'm sorry I lied."

His touch warmed my arm. Warmed my soul, even. I didn't understand it. I fought it. But I felt it all the same.

He dropped my arm.

As I walked away, the truth about us became obvious.

We'd either end this thing madly in love or dead by the other's hand.

In the crowd of the wounded, I found Aeri. She looked like hell, her ghost suit dirty and burned, her hair a mess.

"Thank fates." She hugged me tightly, then pulled back. "Are you okay?"

"I'm fine."

"You look like hell."

"In fact, I feel like hell." I looked around. "Is everyone okay? Any casualties?"

"Injuries, no deaths."

My shoulders lightened, as if a thousand-pound rock had been removed from my back. "Oh, thank fates. I can't believe I caused this."

"But you fixed it."

"Barely." The road was still a mess. Everything was.

"But you did. And the Council of Demon Slayers covered for you all the way. No one knows it was you. Not even the Order of the Magica."

"Good." The last thing I needed today was a prison sentence.

"You got your magic under control?"

"Sort of. I can use it, but I need a lot more practice. Met my mom, though."

Aeri's jaw slackened. "No way. What's she like?"

"Total bitch. I'll tell you all about her."

"Can't wait."

"Let's clean up. The road looks like hell."

Aeri nodded. "Then we're going home, getting a shower, and getting a *really* stiff drink."

I slung an arm around her shoulder. "You read my mind."

As we started toward the middle of the road where the asphalt was pressed up in a ridge like a giant scar, I caught sight of Tarron standing on the roof across the street.

Just like the night I'd created this crevasse.

Had he really been watching me that night?

Was he hiding something?

He gave me one last long look, then turned and disappeared. As I watched, a memory tugged at my mind. The vision of the future that I'd had while in the Unseelie Court.

I would kill him one day. Put a dagger right through his chest.

It hadn't happened yet.

Briefly, I'd thought that the scene in my mother's castle had been what I'd envisioned. She'd tried to get me to kill him in the same way. But I hadn't been crying then.

In the vision, I'd cried. And I'd done it. I'd killed him.

I swallowed hard, praying that the vision was false but knowing it wasn't.

THANK YOU FOR READING!

I hope you enjoyed reading this book as much as I enjoyed writing it. Reviews are *so* helpful to authors. I really appreciate all reviews, both positive and negative. If you want to leave one, you can do so on Amazon or GoodReads.

AUTHOR'S NOTE

Thank you for reading *Heir of the Fae!* If you've read any of my other books, you might know that I like to include historical places and mythological elements. I always discuss them in the author's note.

Most of the historical and mythical elements that appear in this series were discussed in the author's note for book one, *Trial by Fae.* There was only one new thing in this one, and if you've read some of my author's notes from the FireSouls' series, you'll be familiar with it, so feel free to peace out now and I hope to see you at the next book!

Now onto the archaeology and ethics bit! (It's more interesting than it sounds, and really important to me since I am also archaeologist). One of the things that I worked hardest on in this series is how Cass, Nix, and Del —owners of Ancient Magic, which Mari and Tarron visit —treat artifacts and their business, Ancient Magic.

Tragically, archaeology isn't quite like Indiana Jones

(for which I'm both grateful and bitterly disappointed). Sure, it's exciting and full of travel. However, booby-traps are not as common as I expected. Total number of booby-traps I have encountered in my career: zero. Still hoping, though.

When I chose to write a series about archaeology and treasure hunting, I knew I had a careful line to tread. There is a big difference between these two activities. As much as I value artifacts, they are not treasure. Not even the gold artifacts. They are pieces of our history that contain valuable information, and as such, they belong to all of us. Every artifact that is excavated should be properly conserved and stored in a museum so that everyone can have access to our history. No one single person can own history, and I believe very strongly that individuals should not own artifacts. Treasure hunting is the pursuit of artifacts for personal gain.

So why did I make Nix and her *deirfiúr* treasure hunters? I'd have loved to call them archaeologists, but nothing about their work is like archaeology. Archaeology is a very laborious, painstaking process—and it certainly doesn't involve selling artifacts. That wouldn't work for the fast-paced, adventurous series that I had planned for *Dragon's Gift*. Not to mention the fact that dragons are famous for coveting treasure. Considering where the *deirfiúr* got their skills from, it just made sense to call them treasure hunters.

Even though I write urban fantasy, I strive for accuracy. The *deirfiúr* don't engage in archaeological practices—

therefore, I cannot call them archaeologists. I also have a duty as an archaeologist to properly represent my field and our goals—namely, to protect and share history. Treasure hunting doesn't do this. One of the biggest battles that archaeology faces today is protecting cultural heritage from thieves.

I debated long and hard about not only what to call the heroines of this series, but also about how they would do their jobs. I wanted it to involve all the cool things we think about when we think about archaeology—namely, the Indiana Jones stuff, whether it's real or not. But I didn't know quite how to do that while still staying within the bounds of my own ethics. I can cut myself and other writers some slack because this is fiction, but I couldn't go too far into smash and grab treasure hunting.

I consulted some of my archaeology colleagues to get their take, which was immensely helpful. Wayne Lusardi, the State Maritime Archaeologist for Michigan, and Douglas Inglis and Veronica Morris, both archaeologists for Interactive Heritage, were immensely helpful with ideas. My biggest problem was figuring out how to have the heroines steal artifacts from tombs and then sell them and still sleep at night. Everything I've just said is pretty counter to this, right?

That's where the magic comes in. The heroines aren't after the artifacts themselves (they put them back where they found them, if you recall)—they're after the magic that the artifacts contain. They're more like magic hunters than treasure hunters. That solved a big part of my problem. At least they were putting the artifacts back. Though that's not proper archaeology, I could let it pass. At least it's clear that they believe they shouldn't keep the artifact or harm the site. But the SuperNerd in me said, "Well, that magic is part of the artifact's context. It's important to the artifact and shouldn't be removed and sold."

Now *that* was a problem. I couldn't escape my Super-Nerd self, so I was in a real conundrum. Fortunately, that's where the immensely intelligent Wayne Lusardi came in. He suggested that the magic could have an expiration date. If the magic wasn't used before it decayed, it could cause huge problems. Think explosions and tornado spells run amok. It could ruin the entire site, not to mention possibly cause injury and death. That would be very bad.

So now you see why Nix and her *deirfiúr* don't just steal artifacts to sell them. Not only is selling the magic cooler, it's also better from an ethical standpoint, especially if the magic was going to cause problems in the long run. These aren't perfect solutions—the perfect solution would be sending in a team of archaeologists to carefully record the site and remove the dangerous magic—but that wouldn't be a very fun book.

I think that's it for the history and mythology in *Heir of the Fae* (not very much this time, I'm afraid!). I think it was probably my favorite to write, and I hope you enjoyed it and will come back for more Mari and Aeri.

ACKNOWLEDGMENTS

Thank you, Ben, for everything. There would be no books without you.

Thank you to Jena O'Connor and Lindsey Loucks for your excellent editing. The book is immensely better because of you! Thank you Eleonora, Richard, and Aisha for you helpful comments about typos.

Thank you to Orina Kafe for the beautiful cover art.

ABOUT LINSEY

Before becoming a writer, Linsey Hall was a nautical archaeologist who studied shipwrecks from Hawaii and the Yukon to the UK and the Mediterranean. She credits fantasy and historical romances with her love of history and her career as an archaeologist. After a decade of tromping around the globe in search of old bits of stuff that people left lying about, she settled down and started penning her own romance novels. Her Dragon's Gift series draws upon her love of history and the paranormal elements that she can't help but include.

COPYRIGHT

Made in the
USA
Columbia, SC